"Jenny, what ⸻⸻? ⸻ ⸻⸻⸻ ⸻⸻⸻ I'm sorry I couldn't call you last night, but Dad took me out for dinner, and it was pretty late when we got home," Mark said.

"Oh. How is your father?" Jenny asked.

"The same. It was good to see him, but we still have trouble getting along."

"Mark, I know you didn't see your father yesterday. I saw you with Francie!" Jenny said with anger in her voice.

Mark's only reply was, "Oh . . ."

Caprice Romances from Tempo Books

A CAPRICE ROMANCE

Love in Focus

Margaret
Meacham

TEMPO BOOKS, NEW YORK

LOVE IN FOCUS

A Tempo Book/published by arrangement with
the author

PRINTING HISTORY
Tempo Original/August 1983

All rights reserved
Copyright © 1983 by Margaret Meacham
This book may not be reproduced in whole
or in part, by mimeograph or any other means,
without permission. For information address:
The Berkley Publishing Group,
200 Madison Avenue, New York, N.Y. 10016

ISBN: 0-441-49630-X

''Caprice'' and the stylized Caprice logo are trademarks
belonging to The Berkley Publishing Group.

Tempo Books are published by The Berkley Publishing Group,
200 Madison Avenue, New York, New York 10016.
Tempo Books are registered in the United States Patent Office.
PRINTED IN THE UNITED STATES OF AMERICA

* * * Chapter One

Have you ever noticed that sometimes when things seem to be at their absolute, rock-bottom worst, and you begin to think that nothing good will ever happen to you again for as long as you live, all of a sudden something really terrific happens, and things don't seem so bad after all? That's the way it was the day that I met Mark. It began as a terrible day. I overslept. Mom yelled at me. I was late for school. I got a D on my first math test. I sat alone at lunch, and I felt more than ever that I would never fit into this new school, or for that matter, in this new town. To make things worse, it was a Friday, and everyone was all excited about the weekend. Everyone but me, that is. When the bell rang after the last class, kids were rushing around talking about their plans. I had no plans, except to go home and continue the endless job

1

of helping Mom unpack. That was why I decided to go to the darkroom and develop some pictures. I just couldn't face another packing box that afternoon.

Whenever I get depressed, I go to the darkroom and work. There's something about watching those hazy images develop into a photograph that makes me forget everything else. I've been taking pictures since I was eight years old. I started with a little Instamatic, and worked my way up to the 35mm Pentax that I got for Christmas two years ago. I've had some pictures in the literary magazine at Roland, my old high school, and last year I got a runner-up in the Lakeland *Herald* photography contest, so I guess I'm not bad, but it seems as if the more I learn about photography, the more there is to learn, if that makes any sense. So, that Friday, when everyone else was happily talking about parties and dates, I went to the darkroom.

I was going to develop a roll that I had started in Lakeland, and had just finished the week before. I had already done the negatives, and had left them in the darkroom to dry. I put the first one under the enlarger, exposed it, and dropped it into the developing solution. It was a picture of my best friend Jody, myself, and two other friends in front of our old house in Lakeland. It had been taken three weeks earlier, on the day before my family had moved from Lakeland to Stromley, Connecticut. I smiled when I first saw it. It had been taken with the self-timer on my camera, and I had had to rush around to get into the picture, so we were all laughing. But as I looked at it, I felt tears coming to my eyes. I guess Lakeland, Ohio, isn't the most glamorous place in the world, but until three weeks ago, I had lived there all my life, and I missed it. I especially missed Jody, and the other friends that I had left behind.

The next few pictures were of my family moving things out of our house. Most of them were funny. There was one of Mom and Dad arguing over whether or not to take Dad's old 78 record collection which they never played, one of my sister carrying a huge stack of love comics which she is convinced will be worth a fortune some day, and one of my little brother Billy trying to entice our cat Elvira into her travel cage with a can of tuna fish. Then there was one of our whole family in front of the new house here in Stromley. I looked at it critically. We looked like a typical family on moving day, all of us in jeans and T-shirts, with boxes and furniture piled all over the place. Billy was in the middle, holding Elvira, and grinning like the ham that he is. Billy is the youngest, a precocious eight-year-old, with blond hair and dark brown eyes. Then there's my sister Molly, fourteen, also blond, with big blue eyes and a sweet, innocent face. Molly is beautiful, but so shy she really seems to be totally unaware of her looks. Then there's me, the oldest, almost sixteen, curly dark hair and dark eyes, medium height, thin. I don't think I'm what you'd call pretty, but Mom says I'm striking looking, whatever that means.

Then there were some pictures of all of us unpacking here in Stromley. One was of Mom and Dad posing like the painting "American Gothic," looking very serious, with Mom holding a mop and Dad a broom. I had finished the roll and was just about ready to go home when there was a knock on the darkroom door.

"Okay," I shouted. "Just a minute." There was a hook lock on the door so no one could come barging in and expose your pictures. I dropped my last shot into the fixing solution and lifted the hook. "C'mon in," I said, wondering who besides me would be coming to the darkroom on a Friday afternoon.

It was Mark, although at the time I didn't know his name. I'd never met him, but I'd seen him in the halls. He was hard to overlook. He had light brown hair and big brown eyes that sort of matched his hair. He had a summer tan that was slightly faded, and his hair still had blond streaks from the sun, so that he looked as if he didn't belong inside the ugly school walls, but should be outside somewhere.

"Hi," he said. "I'm Mark Watson. You're Jenny, right?" I was amazed that he knew my name.

"Right," I stammered. "Jenny Whitlock."

"I know," he said. "I saw you talking to Susan Jennings and I asked who you were."

"Oh." That's me. The conversation kid. I tried to pull myself together and say something that had more than one syllable in it. "Susan's my neighbor. We just moved here three weeks ago."

"I know," he said again. "She told me that too."

"Well, you seem to know all about me. Anything else I can tell you?"

"Well, let's see," he said, smiling. "Do you have a boyfriend? Susan wasn't sure about that."

I couldn't believe it. Here was this incredibly handsome boy asking me if I had a boyfriend, and all I could do was stare at him like a wounded goldfish. I was trying to come up with a witty reply when he went over to the dryer and pulled out some photos of a football game.

"Last week's scrimmage," he said. "I do sports photography for the *Review*." The Stromley *Review* was the school newspaper. I looked through his pictures. They were good shots and I said so. He shrugged. "Susan also told me that you're a pro." I silently blessed Susan. She had come over one day to

introduce herself, and had seen some of my photographs on the wall of my room. I had put them up even
before I unpacked my clothes. They made me feel
more at home.

This time I shrugged. "Well, I try. I've got a lot to
learn though."

"Don't we all?" he said.

I liked the way he wasn't conceited about his work.
He seemed to feel the same way I did. I could tell he
was serious about photography.

"Listen," he said. "If you're going home I'll walk
with you. I told Steve I'd stop by this afternoon."
Steve was Susan's brother. He was in eleventh grade,
one grade ahead of Susan and myself. I figured Mark
was also in eleventh grade.

"Okay," I said, unable to believe my good luck.
"Just let me get my stuff together." I put my pictures
in a folder, grabbed my books, and we left.

"Can I look through these?" Mark asked as we left
the school building and walked down the street toward
my house. I handed him the folder. "They're just some
shots of my family," I said.

He looked through them without saying anything,
but smiling occasionally. When he came to the end he
said, "These are great. I feel as if I already know your
family just from looking at them." He held up the one
of me and my friends in Lakeland. "Who are they?"
he asked. I told him, and he said, "I bet you miss them,
don't you?" I nodded, not trusting my voice for fear he
would know just how much I missed them.

"I know how you feel," he said. "We moved here
two years ago. At first I felt as if I'd never get used to it.
I like it here now though. You will, too, but it's hard at
first."

I couldn't believe it. Someone who actually under-

stood how I felt. I wondered if Mark had had to eat his
lunch alone at the beginning of his first year here. I
couldn't imagine it. He seemed so confident and self-
assured.

It was a perfect fall day. There was still some
warmth to the sun, but the air was chilly and smelled
of burning wood. As we turned up my street Billy
whizzed by us on his bike, clanging his bell when he
saw us.

"There goes the youngest Hell's Angel," I said, and
Mark laughed.

When we reached Susan and Steve's house, Steve
was outside washing his father's car. He threw a rag at
Mark when he saw us and said, "Have you two been at
school all afternoon? What's wrong with you guys?"
He didn't sound surprised to see us together. I guess I
was the only one who was surprised. I stopped for a
minute, trying to decide what to do. I wanted to talk to
Mark some more, but I felt awkward just standing
there.

"Is Susan home?" I asked Steve.

"No, she went shopping with Mom. Knowing those
two they won't be back until they've hit every store in
town."

I laughed. "Well, tell her I stopped by. See you
later."

I waved at Mark and Steve and started toward my
house. I had gone only a few steps when Mark yelled,
"Hey, wait a minute, Jenny," and ran after me.
"Here's your folder."

"Oh, thanks. I forgot all about it," I said.

We both stood there for a minute, and then he said,
"Listen, I'll see you next week, okay?"

"Okay. Have a good weekend," I said.

"Yeah, you too. See you." He ran back up the driveway to Steve's, and I walked on to my house, wondering what he was doing over the weekend. He probably had at least two dates, or else a steady girlfriend whom he was spending every minute with. But why did he want to know if I had a boyfriend? Maybe, just maybe, he wanted to see more of me. Then I told myself I was being silly. Just because a nice friendly guy offers to walk home with a person, there's no reason to jump to conclusions.

I went in the back of the house and immediately began feeling depressed again when I saw all the packing boxes still waiting to be unpacked. Great weekend, I thought. Forty-eight hours of slave labor.

My father is a math professor. He's head of the math department at the University of Connecticut, which is why we moved here. He must be smart, I guess, but you'd never know it to see him around here. When it comes to unpacking, he's pathetic. He takes everything out of one box and puts it in another. Mom and I try to do it when he's not around, because he's really a liability. The other day he was carrying a box of Christmas stuff from one room to another. It was the third time he'd moved it. He tripped over Elvira, dropped the box, spilling everything in it and breaking most of the bulbs. Then he stepped on a piece of broken glass and was hopping around and knocked over a box of books. We decided not to let him help any more after that.

I figured I could get one box unpacked before he got home if I hurried, so I tackled a box marked "misc.," for miscellaneous. It had everything in it from a screwdriver to some of Billy's pajamas. You'd think that after being here for three weeks now we'd be mostly unpacked, but Mom works full time as assistant editor of *Connecticut* magazine, so she doesn't have much time either. I figured maybe if we worked hard this weekend we could wrap it up.

I was just finishing the box when I heard Mom's key in the door. "Hi, sweetie," she said. "Oh, you wonderful child. You got a 'misc.' unpacked. Those are the worst because everything goes in a different place. Dad's not home yet I take it." She asked how my day had gone and I said okay. I showed her the pictures I had developed. She laughed at the ones of Dad and herself. When she saw the one of me and Jody and the others she said, "Aw, do you miss them?"

I nodded. "Today was a pretty good day though," I said. Then I thought about how horribly it had begun, and I smiled. Just thinking about Mark made me feel better. I didn't tell her any of that though.

Dad arrived a little later than usual bearing two large bags of Chinese food. We all sat around the kitchen table and gorged. Most of our meals lately have been sandwiches or carry-out because the kitchen stuff is still being unpacked.

"This weekend I'm determined to get this kitchen organized," said Mom. "Before we all die of malnutrition. What do you say to a marathon day of unpacking tomorrow? I bet we can just about wrap it up if we really work hard."

"I must say I'm beginning to miss the comforts of an ordered life," said Dad. "But unfortunately I promised my students I'd be in the office tomorrow for conferences."

"Oh, dear," said Mom with a wink at me. "Well, darling, the rest of us will just have to carry on without you."

"I'm so sick of unpacking I could die, but there sure

isn't anything better to do around here," said Molly.

Mom gave her a sympathetic look. "It'll get better, sweetie," she said. "It just takes time."

Molly had been miserable ever since the move. As I said, she's so shy that she has a hard time making friends, and I knew she hated our new school. She's never had many hobbies or interests the way Billy and I have, which also makes it harder to meet new people. Mom and Dad are always trying to encourage her to get more involved in things, but so far it hasn't worked.

It takes time, Mom said. That's what Mark had said too. I hoped they were right.

* * * Chapter Two

We did work hard that weekend, and we got almost everything unpacked. Things began to settle, and as furniture was arranged and pictures hung, the new house began to seem more like home. The following week was a good one for me. The best I'd had since we left Lakeland.

Monday when I got home from school, Mom said, "There's one more box for you to unpack. I put it on your bed."

"I thought all my stuff was done," I said.

"Just go see," she said.

I went up to my room and found a wrapped present sitting invitingly on the bed. I ripped the paper off, and found a leather camera case that I'd been admiring when Mom and I had gone shopping. It was something I needed desperately, because it had extra compart-

ments for film, lenses, and filters, and all the other
paraphernalia of photography. It made me feel like a
real professional. I ran down and hugged Mom.

"Thanks, Mom. It's fantastic. But what's it for?"

"To carry your camera and all that equipment. You
always look like a pack rat with film bulging out of
your pockets."

"I know that, but I mean, it's not my birthday or
anything."

"I guess you could call it a thank-you present.
You've been a huge help with unpacking, and Dad and
I are proud of the way you've taken the move. We
know it's not easy being uprooted in the middle of high
school," said Mom.

It made me feel good to know that Mom and Dad
really did appreciate the work I'd done. Somehow,
knowing that I had helped made it all worthwhile.

"I just wish Molly could be more positive. She still
seems so unhappy, and she hasn't made any effort to
make any new friends," said Mom.

"She'll work it out," I said. "It takes time, like you
always say." I didn't feel like talking about Molly and
her problems at the moment.

"I hope you're right," said Mom with a worried
look. "Try to keep an eye on her at school, could
you?"

"Mom, I never see Molly at school. The ninth
graders are in a whole different building from us.
Anyway, I see enough of her at home. She's got to
make her own friends, Mom, I can't do it for her."

"I know, sweetie. I'm not asking you to. Just have
a little patience with her, okay?"

"Okay," I said, but I was already thinking about
how much fun it was going to be taking pictures now

that I had my new case. I was actually looking forward to school the next day so I could show it off.

Another good thing happened the following day. I was getting ready to go to lunch and wondering if I'd have anyone to sit with when Susan came up. "Sit with me," she said. "I've got something to tell you."

We waited in line at the cafeteria. "What is it today?" I asked, eyeing the food. "It looks repulsive."

"The usual slop," said Susan. "Some kind of mystery meat on a stale roll. It's amazing that we're all still alive after eating this stuff every day." We got our trays and threaded our way through the crowd to an empty table.

"Guess what?" said Susan as soon as we were seated. "Steve and I are going to have a party next Saturday. We want you to come."

"I'd love to," I said. "I hope I don't have to bring a date though. I don't know anyone to ask."

"Don't worry about that. Lots of Steve's friends will be there without dates, so there'll be plenty of extra guys. It'll be a good chance for you to meet some people."

We spent the rest of lunch talking about the party and who was going to be there. I was dying to ask if Mark would be coming, but I didn't want Susan to get the idea that I liked him, so I didn't say anything. When lunch period was over I said, "It sounds great. Let me know if there's anything I can do to help get ready." I was excited. It would be fun. Especially if Mark was there.

That afternoon I had my first photography club meeting. One of the first things I had done when school started was to join the photography club. You had to be a member if you wanted to use the darkrooms, and, anyway, I figured it would be a good way to meet people. We met once a week, and this was the first meeting of the year. I wondered if Mark would be there.

I was a few minutes late, so the meeting had already begun when I got there. There were about twenty members. I took the first seat I could find, and then looked around for familiar faces. I saw Mark, but he was whispering something to a guy sitting next to him, so he didn't see me.

Mr. Daniels, the faculty advisor, was talking about the plans for the year, and explaining the rules of the darkrooms. Then he introduced the new members. There were three besides me, and he asked us to tell everyone a little about ourselves. I always hate it when teachers do that. I never know what to say. When my turn came I said I'd been taking pictures since I was eight years old, that I'd just moved to Stromley, and that I was originally from Lakeland, Ohio. It sounded boring, but I've never been good at summing up my life in three sentences. As I sat down Mark smiled and applauded silently for me. I hoped he couldn't see my face. It had turned four shades of red.

Then Mr. Daniels announced a contest that the school system was sponsoring. Each school would have its own competition, and the winner would go to a county-wide contest. It was for a photo essay on a subject of the student's choosing, but it had to be related to school life. It sounded interesting and I decided I would enter if I could come up with a good topic.

When the meeting was over, Mark came over and said, "So, you've been taking pictures since you were eight years old. No wonder you're so good."

I blushed again. Why had I said that? Who cares how long I've been taking pictures. "I hate introducing myself like that," I said. "I always sound like a moron."

He laughed. "You sounded fine to me," he said. I think it was then that I decided he had the nicest smile I had ever seen. He continued to stand beside my desk while I fumbled with my books and camera stuff.

"Are you going to enter the contest?" he asked.

"I think so," I said. "If I can come up with a good idea for the theme. How about you?"

"Doing the sports photography for the paper keeps me pretty busy. I don't think I'll have the time," he said. I finally got everything stuffed inside my book bag and was ready to go. I was just about to say good-bye when he said, "Ahh, I've got the car today. Would you like a ride home?"

"That would be great," I said, trying not to show my excitement and nervousness. Be casual, I told myself. He's only offering you a ride home, not proposing marriage. Let's not jump to conclusions. Still, I thought, he must like me a little.

"I've got a lot to carry tonight, so a ride would be nice," I added, in case I had seemed too eager.

"Do you have your own car?" I asked, as we walked out toward the parking lot.

"Well, I share it with my brother. He's older, so he seems to have it most of the time, but I get it sometimes." He was parked down by the gym, and as we passed the girls' soccer practice we stopped to watch for a minute.

"Do you like sports?" he asked.

"I love to watch, but I'm not very athletic. I do a little running to keep in shape, and I love to swim and play tennis, but I'm not good enough for team sports. How about you?'' I asked.

''Baseball's the only sport I'm good at, but I like tennis and I love to ski,'' he said. ''You know, if you like to watch sports, I have a great idea for the contest. Why don't you do women's sports?''

I thought about it for a minute. Sports in general was too broad, and there would probably be lots of entries in that category, but women's sports was a new angle. I liked it.

''Thanks for the idea,'' I said. ''I just might use it.''

''Well, if you win with it I get a cut of the prize money,'' he said.

I laughed. ''Don't start spending it yet. It'll be a miracle if I even manage to get an entry in on time, let alone winning.''

We came to the parking lot and he pointed to a decrepit gray Volkswagen. ''There she is. The old gray mare. She may not be beautiful, but at least she runs. Most of the time, anyway.''

My house is only a few blocks from school, so we were home in minutes. I was about to get out when he asked if I was going to Susan's party. I nodded. ''It should be fun,'' I said.

''Good,'' he said. ''I'll see you there.'' Then he reached over and pulled one of my curls, gently, not so it hurt. ''I like your hair,'' he said.

I didn't know what to say, so I just stammered, ''Thanks, for the ride I mean, and for the idea.'' Then I got out and watched as he drove off in the ancient little car.

Mom had driven up just behind us, and I was still staring after the Volkswagen when she got out of her car.

''Well, who was that?'' she asked.

"Just a friend, Mom. Don't jump to conclusions," I said.

"Why didn't you invite him in? Now that everything's unpacked we have nothing to hide."

"Well, it's not at that point yet. Maybe later."

"Aha! So he may be more than just a friend."

"Mom!" Teasing Molly and me about our boyfriends is one of Mom's, Dad's, and Billy's favorite sports.

As we walked up the driveway Mom said, "Did anything exciting happen in school today?"

"Well, we had our first photography club meeting," I said.

"Oh? How'd it go?"

"Pretty well. The new people had to introduce ourselves, which was awful, but once that was over it was fine. Our advisor Mr. Daniels announced a photo essay contest. I might enter using women's sports as my theme." We went in the back door and I dumped my books on the kitchen table and looked through the mail. Nothing for me.

"Women's sports," said Mom. "I think that's a great idea. What made you think of that? I didn't know you were so interested in sports."

"Well, actually it was Mark's idea," I said.

"Hmmm. I think I'm beginning to like this boy," said Mom.

"Oh, guess what. Susan Jennings invited me to her party Saturday night. Can I go?"

"She's the one who lives right down the street, right?"

"Right. She and Steve are having the party together."

"Well, that sounds like fun. I don't see any reason why you can't go."

"It starts at eight," I said. "Susan says it'll be a good chance to meet some people."

"I'm glad you're making some friends, honey," said Mom.

I went up to my room to do some homework, but I couldn't concentrate. I thought about what Mark had said about liking my hair. It was a funny thing to say, and I laughed to myself. It seemed as if it had just popped out of his mouth. He had asked if I was going to the party, too. I wondered if he had really wanted to know, or if he was just making conversation. Don't get excited, I told myself. He'll probably show up with a date and won't even know I'm there. Still, I couldn't wait until Saturday night.

I heard Molly in her room next to mine, and since I wasn't getting anywhere with my homework I decided to go in and talk to her for a while. She seemed so down lately. It was strange not sharing a room with her anymore. In Lakeland we had always shared a room, but since this house had four bedrooms we each had our own. I loved having the privacy of my own room, but lately I felt that Molly and I weren't as close as we had been. I knocked on her door, and when she said "come in," I went in and plopped down on her extra bed.

"How come you were so late getting home?" asked Molly.

"I had a photography club meeting," I said.

"Oh. I don't see why you want to spend any more time there than you have to," she said. "It's bad enough that we have to stay until three-thirty." In Lakeland school had ended at 3:00.

"Yeah, but club meetings aren't like classes. You should get involved in some. It's a good way to make friends."

"Have you met any nice kids?" she asked. "The kids in my class are all either snobs or dolts."

"You just think that because you don't know them. It's hard at first," I said.

While we talked I looked around her room. It was so different from mine, just like when we had shared a room. My side was usually messier, I had to admit. Molly is so neat it's sickening. Even now everything was put away and perfectly in place. Her bedspreads were pink with orange flowers, and the only pictures were one of Todd, her boyfriend from Lakeland, and a picture of all of us that I had taken last year.

My room, which I loved, had blue and green India print bedspreads and natural wood furniture. My two plants, a Boston fern, which I was very proud of, and a philodendron, hung in the windows. The walls were covered with photographs, mostly ones that I had taken. It was messier than Molly's room, but it had a lived-in quality that I loved. Mom had let us choose our own furniture and bedspreads, as long as they were within a certain price range. That had made the difference between Molly and me very obvious. Our two rooms were as different as they could be.

We talked until dinner, but somehow I felt that Molly was keeping something inside her. She wasn't as open as she used to be with me. It made me feel sad, and I hoped we weren't losing touch with each other. When Mom called us for dinner I gave Molly a hug, and said, "I know it's not great right now, but I think Stromley will be okay. And, anyway, at least we all still have each other." She didn't say anything, but she hugged me back, and we went down to dinner.

* * * *Chapter Three*

When classes ended the following Friday I was excited about the weekend just like everyone else. There was no time to go to the darkroom that afternoon, and for once I didn't need to cheer myself up by developing pictures. I had given Mr. Daniels my proposal for the contest, but I hadn't heard yet if it had been approved. I knew there'd be plenty of time to work on the project later. Right now there were other things to think about.

As Susan left she waved and shouted, "See you tomorrow."

"Okay," I said. "Call me if you need any help." There were thirty people coming to the party. Some I'd met, but many I'd never heard of. Susan had shown me the list, and I had noticed that Mark's name was there with a check that meant he was definitely coming. That was all I really cared about. I hadn't seen him since the day he had driven me home after photography club, but I had been thinking about him a lot. He seemed to keep popping into my head at odd times, like during math and French. It made concentrating pretty difficult, and I was glad my teachers couldn't tell what I was thinking about as I pretended to be glued to their every word.

It was Molly's birthday, and as I gathered up my books I thought about what to get her. Mom had planned a little family party for her. There would just be the five of us, but Mom was making Molly's favorite dinner, lasagna, and was baking a big chocolate cake. Mom and Dad were giving her a guitar, which I knew she wanted. She can play a little, and has always been musical, so I thought she'd be able to pick it up easily. I decided to stop in the village on my way home from school to find something to give her. There was a little shop with handmade jewelry, so I went in and began poring over the cases of bracelets, earrings, and pins. She had just gotten her ears pierced a couple of months ago, so I decided on a pair of studs in the shape of rainbows, with blue, yellow and red enamel. I was very noble and resisted buying anything for myself, mainly because I couldn't afford it. There were plenty of things I would have loved to have. I heaved a resigned sigh, and went across the street to the drugstore to look for a funny card.

When I got home the house smelled deliciously of garlic and cheese and tomatoes, and I knew Mom had been working on her masterpiece lasagna. I opened the cupboard to get a glass and saw that a chocolate cake had been hidden on the top shelf. I poured myself a Coke and asked Mom if there was anything I could do to help.

"Let's see. Dad's going to make his special salad,

so that leaves the bread, and setting the table. Which do you want?''

''I'll do the bread,'' I said. ''You always overdo the garlic.'' I buttered the Italian bread and left it ready to go in the oven. Then I wrapped Molly's present and put it with the others that Mom had on the table by her chair. Dad was building a fire in the fireplace, and Mom set the table and put little wrapped favors beside each place. Billy came bouncing down the stairs with a big paper bag. ''Can you wrap this, Mom?'' he asked. It was a book of guitar music which I suspected Mom had had a hand in choosing. When Billy picked out presents himself, they were usually something like twenty pieces of bubble gum, or a rubber creepy crawly spider. Mom wrapped his present and put it on the table with the others. There were presents from Grandma and Grandpa, one from Molly's best friend in Lakeland, and one from Aunt Martha, quite a big pile.

Finally everything had been arranged, and Mom shouted up to Molly to come down for dinner. When she saw all the presents at her place at the table, she smiled and said, ''Wow, what a haul. When can I open?''

''Not till dessert,'' said Dad

The lasagna was yummy, and Molly seemed cheerful during dinner. Then Billy brought out the cake, and we all sang Happy Birthday, and Molly began opening her presents. She loved the earrings I gave her, which made me feel good. ''I'll even let you borrow them,'' she said.

''Great, how about tomorrow night?'' I said, teasing her.

Then she opened the one from her friend Ellen. It was a picture of Molly, Ellen, and a few other kids cheering at a softball game last spring. Molly looked at

it for a minute, and then burst into tears. She jumped
up from the table and ran up the stairs to her room.
Mom and Dad looked at each other, and Billy said,
"Wow, she didn't even finish opening her presents."

"I'll go up," said Dad.

But Mom shook her head. "Let's let her be for a
while." We started clearing the table, with no one
saying much. After about half an hour, Molly reap-
peared.

"I'm sorry," said Molly. "I just missed everyone
so much when I saw that picture."

"We all know how you feel, honey," said Mom.
Molly opened the rest of her presents, and then Mom
and Dad gave her the guitar. She loved it, and was able
to play a few songs from the book Billy had given her. I
hoped that the guitar would give her a new interest and
help her to forget her homesickness.

We were all sitting in the living room by the fireplace listening to Molly play when the phone rang. It
was Susan. She asked me to bring some records when I
came tomorrow, and then she said that Mark had been
over seeing Steve, and that he'd been asking questions
about me.

"What sort of questions?" I asked.

"Just curious-type questions, about your family,
and he asked if you were dating anyone. I think he likes
you."

I didn't want Susan to know how much I wanted that
to be true. "He's probably just curious about the new
girl," I said, trying to sound casual and keep the
excitement out of my voice.

"No, it's more than that," she said. "Steve thinks
so, too. Well, I'll see you tomorrow. Don't forget the
records."

I was in a daze when I hung up the phone. Steve

thinks so, too. Those words kept going through my mind until I thought my brain would shut down. Steve should know. He was Mark's closest friend.

I wanted to be by myself so I could think, so even though it was still early I said good night and went up to my room. I tried to think of all the reasons why Mark would ask if I was dating anyone, besides the fact that he wanted to date me himself. He might just be curious, but it didn't make much sense. I couldn't wait until the next day when I would see him at the party. I thought of the other boys I had gone out with, and decided that none of them were nearly as good-looking as Mark. Last summer I had dated a boy named Jimmy Stevens. I liked him a lot at the time, but we had decided to break up when we moved away. It was never serious, and I knew it would never work out long distance. Sometimes I missed him, but I knew it wasn't actually him that I missed, as much as someone to go out with.

It took me a long time to get to sleep that night, and when I woke up the next morning it was nine-thirty, which is pretty late for me. I put on a pair of jeans and a T-shirt, and went down to the kitchen. No one was around. I figured Mom and Dad were out doing errands or something, and Billy was at little league. Molly was probably still in bed. She usually sleeps late on weekends. I fixed my favorite breakfast, a piece of toast with peanut butter on it, and glanced through the paper while I ate. There was nothing interesting in the news, but I read Ann Landers, as I do every day, to see what wonderful advice she was giving to some poor sucker today.

After breakfast I decided I would go over to school to watch the hockey team practicing, and try to get some shots for my photo essay on women's sports. I shouted up to Molly that I was going out, got my camera and some extra film, and headed for school. I was almost there when the old gray Volkswagen whizzed past me, screeched to a stop, and backed up.

"That camera case looks pretty heavy. Want a ride?" asked Mark.

"Sure, if you're going to school," I said.

He nodded and said, "I'm going to run some laps on the track, and then pick up the prints I left there yesterday. Hop in."

I climbed in the car, silently thanking Mom for my new camera case. I probably still looked like a klutz, but at least I didn't have film and stuff bulging out of every pocket and dropping all over the place.

"What's your excuse for going to school on a Saturday?" he asked as we drove toward the campus.

"I'm going to take some pictures of the women's hockey team practicing. I decided I liked your idea of doing women's sports for the contest."

"Wow, that's great. I bet you'll at least make it to the county-wide competition. And when you win, just remember who gave you the idea."

"I haven't even begun taking pictures for it yet. Let's not jump to conclusions," I said, laughing.

He pulled into the student parking lot, and we got out and walked toward the gym complex. He was dressed in running clothes, a blue T-shirt and white shorts, and I watched the muscles in his legs working as we walked along. "Do you run a lot?" I asked.

"Oh, about three or four miles a couple of times a week. I'd like to do more, but it's hard to find the time."

"I know what you mean."

"Do you run?" he asked.

"A little. The most I've ever done is three miles."

"We should run together sometime."

"Well, if you don't mind going at a nice sedate pace, I'd love to, sometime."

"Great," he said. We had reached the girls' hockey field, and he stopped to watch with me for a minute. "They've got a good team this year, I hear," he said. "Well, I'd better get moving. I'll see you tonight."

"Thanks for the ride." I watched as he walked off toward the gym, and then I sat down on a bench at the edge of the field to load my camera. It was a good day for taking pictures. The sky was overcast, which would keep the pictures from being too shadowy. I had just put the new roll of film in the camera when Mark came back again.

"In case you think I'm following you, you're right," he said. "Actually, I wanted to know if you'd like to have lunch with me when you're finished taking pictures."

"I'd love it," I said. "What time?"

"Let's meet by the car in two hours. Will that give you enough time?"

"Perfect," I said. "By then I'll be starved, and I can't take pictures on an empty stomach."

"Certainly not." He laughed and waved as he ran off toward the track. I felt like running too, or possibly jumping for joy. Lunch with Mark, I thought. I hope I'm not too nervous to eat. I tried to calm down and concentrate on taking pictures. I watched the practice for a few minutes before beginning to shoot. I saw a couple of kids from my class, and I waved. Marcie Johnson, a girl in my history class, came over and asked if I was taking pictures for the newspaper. I told her what I was doing, and asked if she thought the coach would mind. She said she was sure it would be all right. She took me over and introduced me to the coach. The coach loved my idea of an essay on wom-

en's sports, and offered to help in any way she could.
She said to take all the pictures I wanted, but to be sure
to stay out of the players' way. I put on a telephoto lens
and began snapping away from the sidelines. I had
used up almost two rolls and had gotten what I was sure
would be some good shots when I glanced at my watch.
Two hours were almost up. I didn't want to be late for
my first date with Mark, so I put my camera away and
started walking toward the parking lot.

I was nervous. I would probably do something incredibly dumb, like pour ketchup all over my plate, or
knock my Coke over. I hoped my nervousness
wouldn't show too much. The more I thought about it,
the worse it got, and by the time I reached the car I was
a wreck. Mark was already there waiting. He had
changed to a clean T-shirt and jeans, and looked like
he'd just gotten out of the shower.

"How did it go?" he asked as I got in the car. "Did
you get some good ones?"

"I think so. It's hard to tell, but I have a good feeling
about some of them."

I noticed that he was holding a folder, and I asked if I
could look through his pictures while he drove. He
handed me the folder and I looked through them
slowly. They were good. There were some great
close-ups of some of the soccer players in the middle of
the game. They really gave me a sense of what the
players were feeling. While I was looking through
them I noticed Mark glance at me and then look quickly
away. I knew how he felt. It's always nerve-racking
when another photographer is looking at your work.
"These are terrific," I said. "You really caught
them."

"Oh, well, thanks," he said, smiling. "They're
really not that good though. The ones you showed me

the other day are a lot better.''

"Ha. That's child's play compared to these. This stop-action stuff is really hard," I said.

"It's easy if you use a fast film and have a good camera. I'm glad you like them, though.''

I had forgotten all about my nervousness while I had been looking at the pictures, but when he asked where we should have lunch it returned again, stronger than ever.

"I don't know any places to eat yet," I said. "So you'd better choose. Just a burger or something is fine with me.''

We went to a place that had forty-one different kinds of sandwiches and hamburgers. It took me a long time to decide what to have, and when I finally ordered a plain hamburger, Mark laughed. "All that deciding just for a hamburger? I thought you were going to have something really exotic.''

"I thought about it, but I have this mad craving for a plain old hamburger, boring as it may sound.''

During lunch we talked about school, and the party, and he told me a little bit about his family. I wanted to ask more but I didn't want to seem as though I was prying. When we finished he paid the bill, even though I tried to pay for myself.

"You're a male chauvinist. I bet you don't believe in women working either.''

"I asked you to lunch, so I should pay. Next time you ask me, and you can pay. We'll go to Chateau Marquand.''

I laughed. Even I knew that Chateau Marquand was the most expensive restaurant in town. "On my allowance it will be five years before I can save enough to take anyone there.''

"That's okay. I can wait," he said. He took my

hand and looked at me, and I had the feeling he was
trying to tell me something. Don't jump to conclusions, I told myself. It was just a joke.

When he dropped me off at home he said, "See you
tonight. Don't be late."

"Thanks for lunch," I said. I got out of the car and
ran into the house in a very good mood.

As soon as I got inside Molly said, "Whose car was
that?"

"It was just a friend from school," I told her.

"A boy?" she demanded, as if they were some sort
of exotic species.

"Yes, a boy. He's in the photography club. He took
me to lunch."

"Where'd you eat?" she asked. I didn't know why
she was suddenly showing such an interest in my social
life. I thought it might be because she was jealous.

"The Burger Bank. They have forty-one different
kinds of hamburgers."

"Yuck. How gross," said Molly. She had recently
decided to become a semi-vegetarian, but I noticed that
she still wolfed down steak whenever we had it.

"Isn't that the boy I saw you drive home with the
other day?" asked Billy.

"Maybe, but why are you all cross-examining me
like this? What's it to you?"

Billy began singing. "Jenny's got a boyfriend. Boy
is he ugly. He must be weird if he wants to go out with
you."

I walked coldly up to my room trying to preserve
some dignity.

* * * Chapter Four

Susan's party didn't begin until eight, but I started getting ready at six. I was too excited and nervous to eat any dinner, and besides, we were having leftover lasagna, and I didn't want to smell like a pizza parlor.

I love taking long hot baths, so I filled the tub and poured in plenty of scented bubble bath. I didn't stay in too long because I didn't want my skin to get all wrinkly and prunelike the way it does if you take a really long bath. (I've been known to stay in the tub for seventy-six minutes. Billy timed me.) After my bath I washed my hair and blow dried it. It's so curly that I've never had to set it or anything, which is good, except that I'm never sure how it will turn out. Sometimes, after I blow dry it, it looks perfect, but other times it comes out all lopsided which makes me so mad

I feel like chopping it all off. Mom says that no one notices this but me, but they'd have to be blind not to notice it. I always think that the way my hair comes out is an omen for the night. If it comes out well, it will be a good night, if not, disaster. Luckily that night it turned out pretty well.

Then I had my usual problems trying to decide what to wear. If I'd been in Lakeland I probably would have worn jeans and my favorite sweater, but kids here seem to dress up a bit more, so I decided on a pair of corduroy slacks and my new blouse.

I was ready an hour early, and of course the time crawled by. I picked out some records to take, and then watched TV with Billy. At eight I began looking out the window to see who was arriving. I hadn't seen Mark, but after about ten people had gone in I couldn't wait any longer. I said good-bye to Mom and Dad and walked over to the party.

When I first arrived there was hardly anyone there that I knew. I got an attack of nerves, and wished I could just go home and forget the whole thing. The party was downstairs in the Jennings' game room. It's a nice big room with a fireplace in which a roaring fire crackled. Everyone was standing around the stereo or the table where Cokes, pretzels, and potato chips were waiting to be consumed.

Susan came over to me with a girl named Karen and introduced us. I talked to Karen for a while, until her boyfriend came over and asked her to dance. A few other couples began dancing, and more people were arriving. I was beginning to feel very conspicuous. It seemed as though everyone knew each other except me. I wondered where Mark was. I decided to get a Coke so at least I would look like I was doing something. I walked over to the refreshment table, and a guy right beside me opened a can. It sprayed, and a little went on my arm, but not enough to make any difference. The boy who had sprayed me said, "Oh, I'm really sorry. Wait, let me get a napkin." He grabbed a handful of paper napkins and began mopping at my arm like mad, even though it was hardly wet at all.

"I'm really sorry," he kept saying. "I'm such a klutz."

"Don't worry. You hardly got me at all," I said, trying to make him feel better. "Anyway, it's not your fault that someone shook the can."

"Hey, you're in my math class, aren't you?" he said. He looked familiar, and now I remembered where I had seen him before.

"I guess so. I'm usually half asleep in that class, so I'm not too observant," I said.

"I know what you mean," he said. We talked about school for a while. He seemed nice, and I was glad that at least I had someone to talk to, but I kept thinking about Mark, and wondering why he was so late.

Richard, the boy who had spilled the Coke on me, asked me to dance. I didn't really want to, but it seemed mean to say no, so we joined the other couples on the floor. I watched him as we danced, and I could tell by the way he moved that he was shy. He wore glasses and had dark, wiry hair, and a nice lopsided smile. I couldn't help but like him, but I felt none of the attraction I had felt for Mark the first time I'd seen him. We danced two dances, and then I wanted to get something to drink. One thing I hate about dancing is that sometimes it's hard to know when to stop. If someone asks you for a dance, do you stand there when it's over, or what? I always feel awkward. It seemed as though Richard would have been happy to go on dancing all night, but I wanted to get a better view of the stairs, so I could see Mark when he came in. We went back to the refreshment table. I had a Coke which Richard poured. "This time I promise I won't spray you," he said.

Then I saw Mark. He was sitting in a corner across the room talking quietly to a girl. He must have come in while I had been dancing. Richard was saying something, and I realized with a start that I hadn't heard him. "Sorry," I said. "I was thinking about something else."

"I was just noticing Mark and Francie," he said, nodding toward Mark and the girl. "Maybe they're going to get back together after all."

I watched them for a minute. They were talking very seriously. Francie had long blond hair and what looked like a perfect figure.

"Did they go out together?" I asked Richard, trying not to seem overly curious.

"For two years. They broke up last summer when Francie met some guy at the camp where she worked. Apparently Mark was really blown away."

All of a sudden I felt my excitement drain away. I could tell that Mark still liked her. I watched the intense way he looked at her as they talked. I wondered if he was trying to convince her to come back to him.

"Excuse me," I managed to mumble to Richard, and I stumbled up the stairs and out the back door before anyone noticed. I hoped maybe Richard would think I'd just had to go to the bathroom or something. I sat on the back steps for a minute, trying to decide if I should go home, or if I should go back downstairs. I had been sitting there for a few minutes, and had just about decided I couldn't face going back down, when Mark sat down beside me.

"Hi," he said. "I was wondering where you'd disappeared to so fast. Too hot for you downstairs?"

"I just needed some air," I said.

I wasn't sure what to say next, but Mark said, "Sorry I was late getting here. There were a few problems at home. You seemed to be having fun anyway."

"I don't know many people, but it's a good chance to make some new friends."

"Oh, like Richard Black?" he asked.

I looked at him. I wasn't sure if he was joking or if he was a little bit jealous. There were all kinds of things I wanted to ask him, like what was going on between him and Francie, and what kinds of problems he had at home, but I didn't want to seem as though I was prying. I decided just to let it be, and to try to have a good time.

"Richard's nice, but a few dances with him were plenty," I said.

"How about a few dances with me?" he asked. "Are you ready to face the mob scene again?"

"Sure," I said, and when I looked at him I felt as though I could dance for a week straight, and never get tired.

We went back downstairs and danced for a while, until we collapsed on the couch to rest. Susan and her boyfriend Tony were sitting next to us, and she leaned over and whispered, "I think I was right about Mark. Looks like you two are having a good time together."

I nodded. "It's a great party," I said, and then the music started again, and it was impossible to talk.

We sat for a while, sipping Cokes and watching the dancers. I noticed that Richard was dancing with Amy Cooke, a friend of Susan's, whom I had gotten to know quite well. They seemed to be having a good time together, and I was glad. Then I saw Francie dancing with a tall guy I didn't know. I snuck a glance at Mark and saw that he was watching her too. She was laughing loudly and twirling around, occasionally bumping into someone and sending them flying. No one seemed to mind a bit, or even to notice. When the music stopped, she threw her arms around the guy she was with. He got them both a Coke, and then they disappeared into the crowd and I couldn't see them anymore. Mark and I danced some more, and then Susan came downstairs with a plateful of hot dogs. Everyone crowded to the food table and began stuffing themselves as if they hadn't eaten in two weeks. After each of us had two hot dogs, Mark said, "I feel like I need a walk after all this food. Want to go outside for a while?"

I wondered if a walk was really what he had in mind. The truth was, my experience with kissing was pretty limited. Jimmy and I had done our share, but that was all, and I had only kissed one other boy besides him. Part of me was dying to kiss Mark, but the other part of me was scared.

I hesitated for a minute, and then I said, "Okay, I could use some fresh air."

He took my hand and led me through the crowd of dancers and upstairs. We found our coats and went out the back door. The cool air felt good.

"Almost a full moon," said Mark as we walked around the side of the house and out onto the street.

"Which way shall we go?" he asked.

"That way," I said, pointing away from my house.

"It's a good party," he said. "Are you having fun?"

I nodded, and he smiled and said, "I told you you'd get to like it here."

I smiled and thought to myself that if every night could be like this I'd get to like it very quickly. We walked around the block, and then he led me to a little bench in the Jennings' back yard.

"Let's sit here for a minute before we go in," he said. We sat down, and he said, "Steve told me that he and Susan used to pretend this bench was a boat in the middle of the ocean when they were kids."

"That sounds like Billy," I said. "He's always pretending something like that."

"I wouldn't mind if it was a boat, right now. Would you?"

"It might be sort of cold," I said, laughing.

"I know a great way to keep warm," he said, and he took my face in his hands and kissed me. In a minute he looked up and said, "I've wanted to do that all night. In fact, ever since we met, that day in the darkroom."

He put his arms around me and kissed me again, and this time it seemed to last forever. I forgot about everything else except the feeling of his lips on mine, and his arms around me.

I'm not sure how long we stayed there on the bench, but after a while we heard voices at the back door.

"We'd better go back in," I said. "They'll think we've been kidnapped or something." We walked toward the house, holding hands. A couple was coming down the back steps, and when we got closer, I saw that it was Francie and the boy she'd been dancing with. Mark saw her too. He stopped and dropped my hand. He seemed about to say something to them, but they hadn't seen us and they wandered on out into the yard. As we went up the steps to the house I wondered what he had been about to say.

We went back into the party and danced a few more times before it was time to go home. Most people had already left when we finally said good-bye to Susan and Steve. As we left, Susan said, "I'll call you tomorrow." I figured she wanted to hear about Mark and me.

Mark walked me home and gave me one last kiss at the door. "I had a great time tonight," he said.

"Me, too. I think I really am getting to like it here."

"I'll call you tomorrow," he said as he went down the steps.

I went inside, locked the door, put the lights out and knocked on Mom and Dad's door to tell them I was home. As I was getting ready for bed, I thought about everything that had happened that night. I didn't know what was going on with Mark and Francie, but I was pretty sure Mark liked me, and I knew one thing for certain, and that was that I liked him more than any boy I'd ever known.

* * * *Chapter Five*

      The phone rang at 9:30 the next morning. I was just getting up, and I could hear Molly grumbling in her room about rude people who call early Sunday morning. I crossed my fingers, hoping it would be Mark. Mom answered it and then shouted up that it was for me. I ran into the hall. Please let it be him, I thought, but I told myself it was probably Susan because I didn't want to get my hopes up. I grabbed the phone and then put my hand over the mouthpiece. I took a deep breath and told myself to relax. I didn't want to sound as if I'd been waiting for the phone to ring.

    "Hello," I said, trying to sound as if I got calls from boys every Sunday morning of my life.

    "Hi. Did you sleep well?" It was him! I felt a thrill

of happiness rush through my body when I heard his voice.

"Hi," I said. "I slept all right, I guess."

"Oh. I hardly slept at all. I was too busy thinking about you. I just called to tell you that if I flunk my history test tomorrow, it's all your fault. I have to study all day, and since I got no sleep last night I feel about as much like studying as going to the moon. What are you going to do today?" he asked.

"Well, I might go over to Susan's and see if I can help clean up. That was a good party."

"I had a great time. I just wanted to tell you that," he said.

"Me, too," I said.

"Well, think of me as I slave away. I'll see you in school."

"Okay. Thanks for calling." I hung up the receiver and went back to my room. I was wide awake, and couldn't possibly have gone back to sleep, but I lay down on the bed anyway. I just wanted to savor the fact that a beautiful boy like Mark hadn't been able to sleep last night because of me. I wondered if Francie had ever kept him awake, and then I tried to put her out of my mind. I closed my eyes and imagined him sitting at his desk trying to study. Was he thinking of me right now? I wondered.

After a while I got dressed and went downstairs to have some breakfast. Mom and Dad were both up. Dad was puttering around in the kitchen, and Mom was sitting in the den reading *The New York Times*, exactly as they do almost every Sunday. Dad isn't much of a cook, except for a few specialties, and Sunday breakfast. I have to admit he's great on Sunday breakfasts. He always makes an elaborate brunch for everyone. He also makes a huge mess in the kitchen which he bribes

Molly and Billy and me to clean up after brunch is over. Mom never goes near the kitchen on Sunday morning. "The whole thing is his problem," she always says.

In fact, most Sunday mornings Mom sits in the den surrounded by newspaper. She loves the Sunday *Times*. No one else is allowed to touch it until she is done. As she finishes each section she throws it on the floor, and then it's up for grabs. We always tell her she shouldn't be so possessive, but she says it comes from being the youngest of four children.

Anyway, this Sunday was no different from any other, except that Mom was exhibiting a great amount of curiosity about who had called this morning. She was trying to be casual and not seem overly curious, but I could tell she was dying to hear all about it.

"How was the party?" she asked.

"Oh, fun," I said, glancing through one of her discarded sections.

"Lots of nice people?"

"Um hmmm."

"Anyone in particular?"

"Oh, maybe."

"Was that nice boy who brought you home the other day there?"

"You mean Mark?"

"Yes, I think that's what you said his name was. The one who gave you the idea for doing women's sports."

"Yes. He was there."

Mom decided she wasn't going to get anything out of me that way, so she went back to her paper. But after a while she looked up again. "By the way," she said. "Who was on the phone this morning?"

"Just a friend," I said.

"Well, I had assumed it was a friend. I was wondering if it was any friend in particular."

"Why is everyone around here always cross-examining me? What's this sudden fascination with my social life?" I asked.

"Goodness. I'm just trying to show a little motherly interest. But if you wish to keep it all a deep, dark secret, far be it from me to interfere." She went back to her paper with an air of righteous indignation.

Part of me wanted to tell Mom all about Mark, but part of me wanted to keep it all to myself for a while too. I've always been able to talk to Mom easily, and as I've said, we're pretty close. But for some reason I wasn't ready to tell her about Mark yet. I knew she was a bit hurt, so I tried to change the subject. "Breakfast smells great," I said.

"Mmmm," she said, absorbed now in her paper. I tried to concentrate on the article I was reading but my mind kept shifting to last night and to Mark. I couldn't wait until school when I would see him again. Since he's a grade ahead of me we don't have any classes together, and my lunch period is the period before his, but there was always photography. I knew at least I'd see him in our club meetings, if not before. I sat dreaming about next week, and pretty soon Molly came stumbling downstairs, looking as if she'd been up all night.

"Can't you tell your friends not to call so early? I couldn't get back to sleep," she said.

"Sorry." I wasn't in the mood for a fight, but it was ridiculous for her to be mad just because I got a call at 9:30 on Sunday.

"You're just jealous because no one ever calls you. Maybe if you made an effort to make some friends you'd get a phone call or two yourself,'' I said.

"There's no one in this town worth talking to, as far as I can see,'' she said.

"There are fifty thousand people in Stromley, and plenty more nearby,'' said Mom. "If you can't find a few nice people out of all those, maybe there's something wrong with you. I'd suggest you try a little harder before giving the town up as a total loss.''

Molly didn't say anything, but picked the paper up and pretended to be engrossed. Pretty soon Dad shouted from the kitchen, "Okay, gang, breakfast is ready.'' We all went into the kitchen and helped ourselves to the sausage, scrambled eggs with cheese, and blueberry muffins that Dad had set out on the counter.

"Mmmm. Looks great, Dad,'' I said as I sat down at the table in the breakfast nook.

"Yeah, except for the sausage. Yuck,'' said Molly.

"By all means don't eat it if it's against your principles,'' said Dad, spearing an extra piece of sausage. "All the more for the rest of us.''

After breakfast Molly and I cleaned up the kitchen. When we were done, she said, "Want to hear a new song I learned on my guitar?''

"I'd love to, later. Right now I've got to go over to Susan's to see if she needs help cleaning up after last night. I left some records over there too, and I want to pick them up before I forget about them. I'd love to hear it tonight though.''

She looked hurt, and I felt guilty, but after all, I had my own life to live. I would listen to her for hours tonight to make up for now. I went downstairs to call Susan. She said most of the cleaning up was done, but to come over anyway. I wanted to talk about the party, so I hurried over to her house. When I got there, Susan was the only one home. Steve had gone out somewhere after helping her clean up, and her parents were at a football game.

"Hi, that was some party," I said when she opened the door.

"Yeah, I'm so glad it turned out all right. I was nervous. I think everyone had a good time, though," she said.

"I sure did," I said. She led me into the kitchen and fixed us both a Coke.

"I noticed," she said. "Looks like I was right about Mark. You're lucky. He's so cute."

"Well, I don't want to jump to conclusions, but I do like him a lot, and I think he likes me. He called this morning just to say hi."

"Wow, he can't even go twelve hours without calling you. Sounds serious."

I wasn't quite sure how much I wanted to tell Susan about the way I felt about Mark. I'd never felt this way about any boy before, and I wasn't sure she'd understand. I liked her a lot, but after all, I'd only known her for a couple of months. Just then Amy Cooke came in, so I didn't have a chance to say any more. The three of us took our Cokes and went downstairs and talked for a long time about the party, and who had danced with whom. Apparently Amy and Richard had had a good time together. I think Amy was hoping that Richard would ask her out soon. Amy is really cute, but slightly overweight. Susan had told me that she had never had a real boyfriend, or many dates. I hoped that things would work out between her and Richard. Susan's boyfriend Tony was a close friend of Richard's, so Susan was determined that this romance was going to work.

"Just think," said Susan. "We can go to the movies

together and everything. Tony will have his license
soon, and we'll really be able to have a good time.''

Tony and Richard were both sophomores, a year
younger than Mark. He did seem older than the boys in
our class, which I liked, but which was also a little bit
scary. Sometimes I felt as if I should act older when I
was around him.

Amy and Susan and I talked for the rest of the
afternoon, until Amy and I decided we'd better get
home. When I said good-bye I realized that neither of
them really understood how I felt about Mark. I wished
my friends from Lakeland were here. They knew me so
well and would understand perfectly. I told myself that
I was lucky to have friends here at all, and that I was
just feeling sorry for myself. After all, Susan and Amy
were both nice. I just hadn't known them as long as I
had known my old friends from Lakeland.

When I got home I decided to write a long letter to
Jody. I told her all about Mark, how I had met him, and
the party, and Francie, and everything. It felt good to
pour my heart out to someone I knew would understand. It was a long letter, and when I finally finished it
I realized how late it was. I still had to do my history
assignment and study for a math quiz. I worked on my
homework until I was so tired I couldn't see straight.
Just as I was about to turn off the light and go to sleep I
remembered my promise to Molly. I could hear her
strumming away in her room, practicing the new song
she had wanted me to hear. I knew I should go in and let
her play for me, but I was too tired. I told myself that I
wouldn't have made much of an audience, and that I'd
make it up to her next week.

I realize now what a mistake that was, and how
selfish I was being. If I had only paid more attention to
Molly, and tried to help her, we might have avoided a

lot of pain. But I was too wrapped up with my own problems and my relationship with Mark to realize just how unhappy Molly was. One thing I learned that fall is that when someone you love needs you, you'd better be there for them. And they don't always advertise it with a neon sign.

* * * Chapter Six

      I had signed up to use the darkroom on Tuesday afternoon. One thing I've learned is that although it's nice having a large and enthusiastic photography club, it's not so great when there are only two small darkrooms for everyone to use. My dream of someday having my own darkroom was becoming an obsession. In order to get prime-time, from 3:30 to 5:30 after school, you had to sign up at least a week ahead of time. So Tuesday was the first chance I had had to develop since the day I had met Mark.

      I had developed the negatives from the previous Saturday, the ones I planned to use for the contest. I still wasn't sure if Mr. Daniels would pass the idea, but I liked the subject and was excited about it.

      When I first looked over the negatives I was disappointed. It's always hard to tell what the pictures will be like when you take them. Sometimes I have a feeling they'll be the best thing I've ever done, but when you actually see them, they turn out to be rotten. You think you've caught someone just right, and then you find out they moved just as the shutter snapped. Those are the things you can't know until you see the negative. But negatives can be deceiving, too. You can't see the fine details that are often the things that make a good picture great. I dried the negatives quickly and started to print them. Most of them were mediocre at best. I could see I needed a lot of practice on stop-action shots. Some great moves that I had tried to capture had turned out to be nothing but a blur. It was disappointing, but this was a new area of photography for me, and it would take time to get it right. There were two pictures on the roll that I was really proud of though. One was of the team's captain making a beautiful kick almost in midair. The timing was perfect. And the other was of one player watching as her opponent scored a goal. The first one could see what was about to happen, but couldn't do anything about it. Her face showed the frustration that is so much a part of sports.

After developing that roll, I realized what a really talented photographer Mark was. I had seen more of his work in the paper, but it's like anything else, you never realize how difficult a thing is, or how much is involved, until you try to do it yourself. I knew he was good, but now I understood just how good he really was. I was embarrassed to show him this roll, except for the two pictures that had come out well.

When I saw him in photography club the next day, he asked me if I'd had a chance to develop them yet. I showed him the two I was proud of.

"These are great," he said. And I could tell he meant it. "Where are the rest?" he asked.

"Not so good," I said. "This action stuff is a lot harder than it looks. I'm not so sure I'm ready for this yet."

"You can't expect every picture to come out well," he said. I take a couple of rolls of every game just to get a few good shots for the paper. These are great. If I had two shots like these on one roll, I'd be proud."

His words made me feel better, but I still wasn't sure if I should stick with the project. Then Mr. Daniels started to speak about the contest. He said he hoped it would be a chance for us to challenge ourselves, and to try something we hadn't done before, to work on new techniques and new types of photography. Well, I figured I'd sure be doing that if I stuck to the women's sports thing, so I made up my mind to try it. He passed back our proposals, and on mine he had written, "Good idea. I'm looking forward to seeing the results." Me, too, I thought. I just hope they're better than the first roll. Then Mr. Daniels set up conferences with each of us to discuss the project and to help with format ideas. I showed Mark what he had written on my proposal, and Mark wrote, "I get half the prize money," on a scrap of paper. I knew I was going to have to work hard on this project.

After the meeting Mark asked if I wanted a ride home. He seemed preoccupied, but when he stopped to let me out, he said, "I really had fun last Saturday."

"Me, too," I said, hoping he was going to ask me for a date.

"I've been looking for you at school. Have you been hiding from me?" he said with a smile.

I laughed, thinking about how all week I'd been hoping I'd run into him. "I guess our schedules are just different," I said.

"I'm eating my lunch early tomorrow because I'm

going to Westport with the team to take pictures. I'll look for you,'' he said.

"Okay. That sounds good," I said. "Thanks for the ride." I got out of the car, and he waved and drove away, still with a slightly preoccupied air. I couldn't help but wonder if he was thinking about Francie.

I went inside and shouted that I was home. There was no answer, but I heard Molly's voice, so I assumed that she was on the phone. Good, I thought. Maybe she's finally made some friends here. I snooped around the kitchen for a while, trying to figure out what we were having for dinner, and in a few minutes Molly came down.

"Hi," she said. "How come you're so late getting home?"

"I had photography club," I said.

"Who brought you home? Mark?" she asked.

"Ummhmmm." I wondered how she knew Mark's name. I hadn't talked to her much about him.

"Sounds like things are getting pretty serious between you two," she said.

"Well, I do like him a lot. In fact, more than I've ever liked anyone before. I don't know if he feels the same way, though. I don't want to rush things." It felt good to talk to Molly the way we used to when we were back in Lakeland. "Who was on the phone?" I asked her.

"It was Ellen. I felt lonely this afternoon, so I called her. Also, I haven't heard from Todd in two weeks. I wanted to find out if she knew why he hasn't written."

"What did she say?"

"Just that he's been busy with the team lately. She said she's sure he still likes me. I'm so glad I called. I feel much better now."

"Mom and Dad might not be so glad when the bill comes in," I said.

"I'll pay for it myself if they get upset. I might call Todd sometime soon too. They can't expect us just to forget all about our old friends and never talk to them again, can they?"

"No, but there is such a thing as a pen and paper."

"It's so hard to communicate in a letter, though," she said. "I feel as though I hardly know Todd sometimes when I read his letters, but I know that's silly."

"Well, you only went out with him for two months before we moved. Maybe you should try to stop thinking about him so much and concentrate on meeting some new people. Long-distance romances don't usually work out, you know."

"Oh, no, not you, too," she said. "Everyone around here is determined to convince me I don't love Todd. No one understands. Just because you never met anyone you really care about. Obviously you and Jimmy didn't have what Todd and I do, or you wouldn't have broken up so easily."

"Well, that may be, but you could still see other people, couldn't you?"

"I haven't met anyone here worth talking to, let alone dating. See you later."

A few minutes later I heard her up in her room strumming her guitar. I knew it was shyness that made Molly put up a barrier around herself, and pretend she didn't like anyone else, but I also knew that if she didn't change her attitude she'd never make any new friends. I was worried. She wasn't her old self at all, and I missed her. I just didn't know what to do. I didn't want to talk to Mom about it, because she was already worried enough about her. I went up to my room to start my homework, and pretty soon I had forgotten all about Molly's problems. My math homework was particularly bad. I spent an hour trying to figure out the equations that were assigned. Math has always been hard for me, and this year was worse than ever. My teacher, Mr. Tanner, was the type who should have been writing textbooks instead of teaching. Every time he opens his mouth he spouts equations, but he never really explains anything. As Susan said, he even looks like a computer. When we ask questions he just says, "Keep at it. The light will dawn." But somehow the light wasn't dawning. I was as much in the dark as at the beginning of the year. Richard Black had mentioned that he liked math, so I decided to ask him if he knew what was going on.

I sat at my desk and stared at my paper, getting nowhere. Pretty soon I was staring at the photographs on my wall. I tried to imagine how I would take a picture of Mark. He'd make a great subject. I'd definitely want to get him smiling, but one with his sort of puzzled look would be good too. I realized I wasn't getting anywhere with my math, so I decided to go to bed and forget about it until tomorrow.

Math class is right before lunch. I had hoped that Mr. Tanner would explain things, but I was still totally confused when class was over. We had a test coming up in a week, and I was getting worried. Richard was sitting beside me as he had ever since Susan's party. "How's it going?" he asked.

"Terrible," I said. "I'm going to flunk this test next week if I don't figure out what's going on. Right now it's about as clear as pea soup. Do you understand this stuff?"

"Well, sort of. If you want I'll try to explain it to you at lunch."

"Oh, that would be great. I'm really getting worried. Tanner just doesn't explain anything."

"Well, I'll see what I can do. C'mon. Let's go to lunch and work on it."

I was so grateful to Richard for taking time at lunch to help me with math that I forgot that Mark had said he would look for me. Richard and I got our trays and stood in line.

"Looks as appetizing as ever," he said, dishing something that was supposed to be lasagna onto his plate.

"I think I'll stick to a sandwich," I said. "It's safer. You're risking your life trying that stuff."

"That party was really fun last weekend," I said.

"Yeah, it was okay," he said. He didn't sound very enthusiastic. I wondered if he wasn't as crazy about Amy as she was about him. I hoped for her sake he was.

We found a table away from the others so we could make some attempt to concentrate. He took out his homework from last night and began going over what he had done, and explaining why. I tried to explain what it was that I didn't understand.

"I still don't see how you know that this x equals that y. It just doesn't make sense to me. I'm retarded when it comes to this stuff."

We worked all through lunch, and I was finally beginning to catch on when the bell rang. I felt much better.

"I think if I go home and work some more on it I'll be able to do tonight's homework. The light is beginning to dawn," I said, mimicking Mr. Tanner.

"You ought to be a teacher when you grow up," I said. "You explain it a lot better than he does. Anyone who can get through to me is a born teacher."

"Well, if you get stuck, just give me a call," he said as he gathered up his books and papers and got ready for the next class. "Explaining it to someone else makes it clearer in my mind too."

"See you later," I said as we dumped our trays and headed in opposite directions.

On my way to my locker I heard a familiar laugh. I looked around, and there was Mark in the midst of a group of eleventh graders. Francie was there, too, and it looked as though she had said whatever it was that had made Mark laugh. I felt a pang of jealousy, and suddenly remembered that Mark had said he would look for me at lunch. They moved on down the hall without seeing me, and I went on to my locker. Had he looked for me, I wondered, and seen me with Richard? Or had he forgotten all about it too? Why was he always with Francie?

As I hurried to my English class I was tormented with questions. If only I hadn't needed help with my math I would have eaten lunch with Mark and would probably have a date for this weekend. Instead, I was back where I started, wondering if he still liked Francie. It was all Mr. Tanner's fault. If he had explained things right in the first place, I wouldn't have had to eat with Richard.

I couldn't concentrate at all during English. I tried to listen to what Mrs. Rappard was saying, but I kept seeing Mark laughing at whatever it was that Francie had said. I wished I had long blond hair like hers, instead of my own horrible kinks. He must have been joking when he said he liked my hair.

Suddenly I noticed that Mrs. Rappard was staring at me.

"Jenny, can you tell us?" she said.

I had no idea what they'd been discussing. I hadn't

even heard the question.

"I had a feeling you weren't quite with us," she said. "Try to keep your mind on English, just for this period. You can think about whoever he is all day long, but not in my class, please."

I blushed and murmured an apology, and tried to keep my mind on the discussion. We were talking about Mark Twain, and the influences that had led him to write *Huckleberry Finn*. I liked Mark Twain, and I liked the class, and Mrs. Rappard was a good teacher most of the time, but even so it was hard to concentrate that afternoon. Susan was sitting beside me and wrote *Mark?* on a scrap of paper. I just smiled when I saw it, but I didn't say anything. I decided I would have to be more subtle. It seemed that everyone knew I liked Mark. It had probably turned him off completely. I became convinced that that was why he had forgotten our lunch and was hanging around with Francie. Then I remembered that I was the one who had forgotten our lunch, not him, and I became more confused than ever. I made a determined effort to pay attention, and finally the class was over.

It was a rainy miserable day out, and when Susan offered me a ride home at the end of the day, I accepted it gratefully. Usually I enjoy the walk, but not on a day like that one.

"You've been pretty quiet lately," said Susan as we walked out to her brother's car. "Is there anything wrong?"

"No, I've just got a lot on my mind. Besides the fact that I'm about to flunk math, everything's fine. This dreary weather doesn't help though."

"I know what you mean."

As we drove out of the parking lot I happened to look back and I saw Mark coming out of the school building followed by Francie. I watched for a minute as they walked together toward his car. I knew they lived near each other, and I tried to convince myself that he had just offered her a ride home to be nice. But somehow I couldn't make myself believe it.

As we drove home I wondered if I should confide in Susan. Steve and Mark were good friends, and she might know if there was anything between Mark and Francie. And it would feel good to talk to someone. Once again I had a longing for my old friends back in Lakeland. Jodie and I had shared everything together. I was sure she would know exactly what to do. When we pulled up in front of my house, I almost asked Susan to come in and talk, but then I decided against it. I just didn't know her well enough yet, and besides, she might tell Steve how I felt about Mark, and then Steve would surely tell Mark. So, when they let me off I simply thanked them for the ride and ran inside out of the rain.

I was surprised to find that Molly was already home. She was lying on the couch with her head hanging over one side, her blond hair almost touching the floor. She was talking on the phone, and looked as happy as I'd seen her look in weeks. Almost like her old self. I went into the kitchen to get a snack, and she continued her conversation for a few more minutes. Finally she hung up.

"Who was that?" I asked.

"Todd," she said. "I just had to talk to him. I left school early. I had a free period last class."

"If you get caught leaving early you'll be in trouble. You know you're not allowed to do that, even if you do have a free period."

"I know, but I just couldn't stand it anymore. I had to talk to him. I miss him so much. He sounded just like his old self. He says he misses me too, and he's going to try to come and see me over Thanksgiving. Wouldn't that be great? Oh, I hope he can come. He's got to come. I don't know if I can live till then.''

"Do you think his parents will let him come all that way? Where would he get the money?''

"I don't see why his parents should mind. He's fifteen years old, and he'd only be gone for a few days. If he can't get the money for a bus ticket, he says he'll hitchhike. It's not that far.''

"Well, don't get your hopes up too much. Thanksgiving is still a month away," I said.

"I know, but he'll get here. I know he will. I hope Mom and Dad won't be too mad about the phone calls. We talked for a long time. I couldn't believe he was home, but he said practice was called off today because of the weather. He said he hasn't written much because he's got so much to do, but he thinks about me all the time. Maybe Mom and Dad won't even notice the extra calls," she said hopefully.

"Ha," I said. "And maybe they'll think Elvira made them. You know Dad goes over the phone bill with a magnifying glass making sure the phone company doesn't cheat us.''

"Well, I'll pay for them myself if there's a problem," she said.

I could have pointed out to her that it would take more than the forty-seven cents I happened to know she had in her piggy bank to pay for the calls she had been making lately, but I didn't feel like talking about her problems anymore. I had enough of my own. I didn't want to hear her raving on about how wonderful it was to hear Todd's voice either, so I took my books and some cookies and went up to my room. I put on my favorite record and lay down on my bed to think.

* * * *Chapter Seven*

I came downstairs just before dinnertime to
see if there was anything I could do to help Mom. She
and Molly had been talking in the kitchen ever since
Mom had come home from work. It was still a rainy,
drizzly day, and it was getting dark earlier than ever
now. The kitchen seemed warm and bright and cozy
compared to the cold and damp outside. Molly had
gone up to her room, but when I came down, Mom
said, "Well, your sister seems-cheerful today. Maybe
she's finally beginning to adjust."

"Maybe," I said, without much conviction. I
wasn't sure if Molly had told Mom about calling Todd
or not, so I didn't mention it. Even though I thought it
was a dumb thing to do, I didn't want to get her in
trouble.

"I had a feeling it would take her longer than you

and Billy,'' Mom continued. "I guess it was just a matter of patience. You can't expect everyone to slip into a new life easily, especially someone as shy as Molly. I must say, I am relieved that she's showing some signs of recovery.''

It seemed to me that Mom was being a bit hasty. The only reason I could see for Molly's improved mood was the fact that she had spent the afternoon talking to Todd on the phone. That wasn't making any progress toward making a new life and new friends here in Stromley. I didn't tell this to Mom, though. She seemed so pleased that Molly was happier, and I didn't want to spoil it for her. I realize now that I should have told her the whole truth, but at the time it seemed silly, and I can't stand tattletales.

At dinner I had to agree with Mom. Molly was like her old self again. She talked and laughed and made jokes, and I realized that I had forgotten how much fun we used to have together. I saw Dad glance at Mom with a pleased but questioning look, and Mom responded with a shrug. I could tell they both thought Molly had finally grown to like our new home, and that night I almost agreed. She talked about her dippy gym teacher, and was really funny imitating her. Then she said she was planning to try out for glee club, and that she'd like to start taking guitar lessons. Dad asked if she had met any other kids who played the guitar. He said maybe they could get together and form some kind of club or group. Molly said she didn't know of anyone else who played, but she didn't act as if his suggestion was crazy, as she would have a few days before. It was so nice to have Molly back to her old self again that I forgot all about my own problems. When the phone rang and it was Mark, I was completely surprised.

Billy answered the phone. "It's a boy," he shouted

to me, knowing I would ask. I jumped up from the table and ran to the den. I didn't need the whole family listening while I talked to Mark.

"Okay, Billy. You can hang up now," I said, and then I said, "hello," in my most composed-sounding voice.

"Hi. This is Mark. Are you having dinner or something?"

"No," I lied. "Hi. How are you?" I wondered if I should say anything about having missed him at lunch. Should I try to explain what had happened? But what if he had forgotten all about it? I decided to wait and see if he brought it up.

"I'm okay," he said. "I just wondered if you wanted to go to the movies Saturday night with me and a couple of other kids."

"Um, Saturday? That sounds great. Let me just ask Mom."

I put the phone down and went back to the dining room to ask if it would be okay. I was so happy. A real date with Mark. I couldn't wait.

Mom said it was fine, and didn't even say I had to be home by a certain time.

I went back to the phone and told Mark I could go.

"Okay. Well, I'll pick you up about seven, if that's okay with you."

"Great. See you then," I said, and we hung up.

He hadn't mentioned lunch, so I decided to forget about it. Whatever had happened, it was past, and however he felt about Francie, he must like me, or he wouldn't have asked me out. It would be our first real date. He had said we'd be going with some other kids. Who? I wondered. Juniors, probably, I thought nervously. I wondered if we would go in Mark's car. I couldn't wait until Saturday.

The following day, Friday, passed quickly. I kept hoping I'd run into Mark, but I didn't see him all day. I was getting ready to go home when Susan came over and said, "Hi. Are you doing anything exciting this weekend?"

"Well, tomorrow I'm going to the movies with Mark, which qualifies as exciting as far as I'm concerned," I said.

"Me too," she said. "That's great. You're lucky. I'm not doing a thing. Tony's going on some dumb fishing trip, so I won't see him all weekend. Why don't you come over tonight if you're not busy? I got some new records I want to play, and Amy said she might come too. She's kind of depressed because Richard hasn't asked her out."

"Well, I may have to baby-sit for Billy, but I think my sister will be home, so I'll let you know. I'll call you, okay?"

"Okay. See you later," she said. On her way out she asked if I wanted a ride home, but it was a beautiful day, so I said I felt like walking. Actually, I was hoping that Mark might drive by.

On my way home I kept seeing things that would have made a great picture. I was furious at myself for being without my camera. It never fails that whenever you have your camera with you, there's nothing to take a picture of, but the minute you're without it there are a million things. I passed a little kid who couldn't have been more than about five carrying a pumpkin that was almost as big as he was. His mother wanted to carry it for him, but he wouldn't let her. He just struggled along behind her lugging this huge pumpkin. He had bright orange hair, and his face was all red from trying to carry it, so he looked like a pumpkin himself. It would have made a terrific picture.

No one was home when I got there, so I sat in the kitchen looking through the mail, and waiting for everyone else. Mom usually got home early on Fridays, but I remembered that Billy had a little league game. I supposed that she had gone to watch. I hadn't been paying much attention to Billy lately, and I felt guilty. I hadn't been to one of his games since we had moved here. I thought about going over to watch, but it was probably almost over, and besides, I realized with surprise that I didn't even know how to get to the school where the games were played. Back in Lakeland I had often gone to his games, and had gotten some good pictures at some of them. The little kids were really cute all dressed up in their uniforms, and so serious about the game. In fact, taking pictures of Billy's games was the only sports photography I had done at all until I started my project on women's sports. It wasn't much, but I was glad I had at least done that.

Soon the back door opened, and Billy came flying in with another boy, both dressed in their little league outfits.

"How was your game?" I asked.

"We slaughtered them. Seven to two. They're terrible."

"Hi. I'm Billy's sister, Jenny," I said to Billy's friend.

"Hi."

"That's Jamey. He's going to spend the night. Mom said it was okay."

"Okay," I said.

Billy and Jamey grabbed some cookies and made a fast retreat up the back stairs to Billy's room. In a minute Mom came in through the garage.

"Hi, sweetie," she said, giving me a kiss on the cheek. "How's everything?"

"Okay, I guess. How was Billy's game?"

"Great. They won, and his little friend Jamey seems like a nice boy. I hope they won't give you and Molly too much trouble tonight. Dad and I have to go to a thing at the university. One of those stuffy faculty parties. I'm sure we won't be late. You're going to be home, aren't you?"

I was rather mad that Mom automatically expected me to be here to baby-sit. I mean, I might have plans for all she knew. Besides, I did want to go over to Susan's.

"Well, Susan asked me to come over," I said. "I might go just for a little while. Besides, Molly will be here, won't she?"

"Yes, but I hate to leave her here all alone with Billy and his friend. If only she had someone to ask over. I don't want to tell you you can't go out, but if you do, try not to be too long. I think Molly could use a little company. Maybe I'll suggest she ask someone over. Where is she, by the way?"

I shrugged my shoulders. Molly usually got home before I did. It seemed like a good sign that she was still at school. But a few minutes later she came in with a package.

"Hi," she said.

"Hi, honey," said Mom. "Where've you been?"

"I stopped in town to get Todd a birthday present. His birthday is next week, and I want to be sure it gets there in time."

I could tell that Mom was disappointed that Molly was still thinking so much about Todd.

"Listen, honey. Dad and I have to go to some

unpleasant faculty thing at the university tonight. Billy has a friend for the night, and Jenny may go out for a while. I wondered if you wanted to ask someone over to help you keep an eye on the boys.''

"That's okay," said Molly. "I was just going to practice my guitar tonight anyway. The boys won't bother me. They'll be glued to the tube all night anyway."

"Well, okay. Jenny will be here most of the time."

I decided to go over to Susan's right after dinner, and only stay an hour or so. I called and told her I'd be over at 7:30.

"Great," she said. "Amy's coming too."

Mom and Dad were going out for dinner, so Molly, Billy and his friend and I had hamburgers in the kitchen. Billy and Jamey were obnoxious as usual, showing off and giggling all through dinner. Molly was quiet, but she didn't seem depressed. After dinner I told her I'd be back in an hour or so, and went over to Susan's.

Amy was already there when I arrived. She was very depressed. When she heard I was going out with Mark tomorrow, she said, "That's great. I sure wish Richard would ask me out."

"Maybe he's afraid to. He always seems kind of shy," I said, though I didn't really think that was the problem.

"Maybe that's it," she said, brightening up.

"I've got an idea," said Susan. "Why don't you have a party and invite Richard? That way he can get to know you better without having to call you for a date if he's shy."

"Do you think I should?" said Amy.

Susan thought this was a brilliant idea, and before

we knew it we were planning Amy's party. She decided to have it the following weekend, which was Halloween.

"Do you think it should be a costume party?" she asked.

"Tell people they can wear one if they want, but they don't have to," said Susan.

Then she got a pen and paper, and we began planning the guest list.

"I don't know many juniors, so I think I'll just invite kids from our class," said Amy. "But if you want to ask Mark, it's okay with me."

"Thanks. Maybe I will," I said.

I was surprised at the way she had been talked into having a party all of a sudden. Susan could be very persuasive.

"Are you sure your parents won't mind?" I asked her.

"Oh, Mom will be thrilled. She's always suggesting I have a party."

We went on planning the party and making up the list, and I forgot all about the time. It was past eleven when I finally remembered that I had told Molly I would be back in an hour. I felt bad and hoped she hadn't been waiting for me. I told Amy and Susan I'd see them in school next week, and went right home. Everything was quiet when I got there. Billy and Jamey were watching TV even though they were supposed to be in bed, and Molly's room was dark, so I assumed she had gone to bed already. Mom and Dad were still out, luckily, so Mom wouldn't know how long I had stayed at Susan's.

I went up to my room and read for a while before I fell asleep too.

* * * *Chapter Eight*

I watched as the gray Volkswagen stopped in front of our drive. Mark got out and walked up the path to our front door. There were two people in the back seat, but I couldn't see who they were. He rang the bell and I answered. I was all ready to go so he wouldn't have to hang around making conversation with Mom and Dad or anything. Billy came running out into the hall as soon as he heard the doorbell, but when he saw Mark he suddenly became shy and didn't say a word.

"Hi," Mark said to Billy while I got my coat.

"Hi," said Billy. "Is that your car?"

"I share it with my brother," said Mark.

"Do you like soccer?" asked Billy.

"I'm not very good at playing it, but I like to watch, and sometimes I take pictures at the games," said Mark.

"You should come to one of our games. They're great," said Billy.

"Okay. I'd like that," said Mark.

"Tell Mom I've gone, Billy," I said. "See you later."

"He's a cute kid," said Mark as we walked out to the car.

"Hmmm. Don't let him fool you," I said.

When we got to the car Mark opened the door for me and said, "Do you know Will and Maria?" I shook my head and he said, "Will Kenner and Maria Dobson, this is Jenny Whitlock." We said "hi," and I slid into the front seat. Mark went around the car and got in on the driver's side. I was glad he was driving. This was the first time I had dated anyone who had his own car, well, almost his own car. Sitting up front beside Mark I felt full of confidence. It didn't matter that I was younger than the others. I felt very grown up.

"You just moved here in September, didn't you?" asked Will.

"That's right," I said, turning a little in the seat so that I could see Will and Maria in back.

"How do you like it so far?" he asked.

"I like it. At first I missed my old friends a lot, but I've met some great people here and I like it."

I was almost surprised to hear myself saying that. A few weeks ago I would have told anyone who asked that I was miserable here. Mark looked at me and smiled. "I told you," he said, almost as if he had read my thoughts.

As we drove to the theater Maria said, "Remember last winter when we went to that horrible movie about the dead who kept coming back to life, and Francie kept imitating that one dead guy all night?"

At the mention of Francie's name my feeling of

confidence exploded like a balloon. I wondered if Mark wished he were with her tonight instead of with me. Apparently Maria and Francie were close friends, and the four of them had double-dated a lot last year. I felt very uncomfortable, as if they were all comparing me to Francie and wishing that she was sitting next to Mark instead of me.

"That had to be one of the worst movies I've ever seen," Mark said, laughing. In a few minutes we reached the theater. Mark parked the car, and then we had to jump out and run to the window to make sure we got there in time. Mark paid for our tickets and then asked if I wanted popcorn. Normally I would have said yes, because I love buttered popcorn, but tonight I was too nervous. I was afraid I might choke on a kernel and croak right there in the theater. The others bought some popcorn, and then we found four seats together and settled down to watch the movie. Mark didn't try to put his arm around me or anything, but every once in a while he would touch my hand and give it a squeeze, and sometimes he leaned over to whisper some comment about the movie. When it was over we went back to the car, agreeing that it had been worth the three dollars apiece that we'd paid to see it.

"Okay," said Will. "Where to now?"

"I'm starved," said Maria. "Anyone in the mood for pizza?"

"You can eat more than any girl I've ever known," Will said. "With the exception of Francie."

"Okay," said Mark. "Pizza it is. Sounds good to you?" he asked, looking at me.

"Great. I love pizza," I said, which was true, and I was hungry since I hadn't had much dinner.

"Let's go to Pete's," said Will. "It'll be crowded, but they have the best pizza in town."

We drove to Pete's Pizza and found a parking place a
few blocks away. "Lucky we have a small car," said
Mark, maneuvering the Volkswagen into the tiny spot.

"I knew it would be crowded tonight," Will said as
we squeezed our way into the restaurant. We had to
wait to get seats, but finally a booth opened up near the
back. We slid in and ordered a large pizza.

"Did you understand what was going on in English
today?" Will asked Mark as we waited for the pizza.

"I don't think anyone did," said Mark. And soon
the three of them were discussing their English teacher
and the class. Mark tried to include me in the conversation, but I couldn't help but feel left out. I wanted to
make some intelligent-sounding comment, but I didn't
even know what they were talking about. I wished that
Mark and I were there alone. When the pizza came I
concentrated on eating, and tried to seem as though I
was enjoying myself. It was delicious, but what happened next caused me to lose my appetite completely. I
heard a loud laugh, and looked around just in time to
see Francie and the guy she was with at Susan's party
come in the door.

"Francie," shouted Maria. "Over here."

Francie and Rob, that was the guy's name, came
over to our table and sat down as if they intended to stay
all night. All of a sudden my stomach felt as if I had
eaten cyanide. I didn't want to make a scene, but I was
so nervous and upset I didn't know if I'd be able to act
normal. Francie was talking, loudly as usual. "You
wouldn't believe the movie we just saw," she said. "It
was all about this planet where the people look like
green blobs, but are really very intelligent. It was
great. Almost as good as that one we saw last winter.
What was the name? Remember?"

"We were just talking about that earlier. I think

you're the only person in the whole world who liked that movie," said Mark.

"Francie's a horror movie freak," Mark explained to me.

"What did you all see?" asked Francie.

We told her, and she said, "Oh, yes, I heard about that one. It sounded deadly. I can't stand that actor. He's such a goody-goody."

One thing I had to admit about Francie, she sure had definite ideas about things, and she wasn't the least bit afraid to express them. I looked at Mark. He laughed when she said our movie had sounded deadly, and I could tell he got a kick out of her. I had the feeling that he was still in love with her.

The conversation often centered around something they had all done together last year, or something the junior class was doing, and I had the feeling that no one, including Mark, cared whether I was there or not. Finally someone noticed that it was 11:45. "We've got to go," said Mark. "If I get picked up for driving after the 12:00 curfew again I'll lose my license until I'm eighteen. Come on, everyone."

We said good night to Francie and Rob and hurried out to the car. "I guess I'll have to drop you off first," said Mark, "since we go right by your house. Do you mind?" he asked.

"Of course not," I said. "I don't want you to lose your license either, you know." But I was upset that Mark and I hadn't had a chance to talk privately all night. When we got to my house he walked me up to the door and gave me a quick kiss.

"Did you have fun tonight?" he asked. "You seemed awfully quiet."

"I'm sorry," I said. "I've just got a lot on my mind. I had a great time. I promise."

"Good. Listen. I was serious about going to one of Billy's games. I bet we could get some great pictures. And anyway, he's a cute kid."

"I'm glad someone thinks so." I laughed. "No, actually that would be great. I've been feeling guilty because I haven't been to one yet this year."

"Okay, I'll call you and we'll figure out when. 'Night," he said, and he gave me one more quick kiss, and then ran back to the car. I hoped he wouldn't get stopped. It was already five minutes past curfew.

I knocked on Mom and Dad's door to tell them I was home, and then went into my room. As I got ready for bed I thought about the evening. The date that I had been so excited about had turned out to be a disappointment. If only I had never heard of Francie. But Mark had kissed me good night, and he had said he would call. The more I thought about it the more confused I became, and yet I couldn't help but think about it. Was it always like this? I wondered. Is this why they say love hurts?

The next morning I asked Billy when his next game was. He said he had one Wednesday afternoon, and next Saturday. Since Wednesday was photography, I told him that Mark and I might come to the one next Saturday.

"Mark's nice. I like him," said Billy.

"Good. Me, too," I said.

But by evening I wished I hadn't said anything. Mark hadn't called. I waited all day, jumping every time the phone rang, and hoping that it was him, but it never was. Mom noticed how jumpy I was and asked what was wrong. "Nothing," I said. I still didn't feel like telling her all about Mark. She had asked how my date was, and I had just said fine, even though I hadn't had much fun at all. I couldn't relax with Mark's friends, especially with Francie. I spent the day brooding about Mark and Francie. I just couldn't get them off my mind.

Finally I decided to do something positive so I wouldn't keep thinking about them. I got out all my old negatives with the intention of sorting them and getting them in order. It was a huge job, and one that I had been meaning to do for ages. I began putting them neatly into special negative folders, clear plastic holders with places to mark the date and subject. The work kept my mind off my troubles for most of the afternoon, but at dinner I couldn't hide the fact that I was worried.

"You sure are quiet today," said Molly. "What happened? Didn't your date with Mark work out?" We were on our way upstairs after dinner, and suddenly I felt like talking to someone about it. I followed her into her room.

"Oh, I don't know," I said. "It was fun, I guess, but I felt out of place with his friends. They're all juniors and have known each other for years. I felt as though I didn't have anything to say to them."

"Now you know how I feel most of the time. That's why I miss Lakeland so much," she said.

I thought about what she said, and I began to understand what she was going through. Poor Molly. If she felt the way I had felt last night all the time, it's no wonder she was miserable.

"But why do you feel like that with kids your own age?" I asked. "They're just as insecure as you are, you know."

"Oh, I don't know. It's hard to explain. I've never been any good at making friends the way you and Billy are. I was finally beginning to feel like I had some good friends, for the first time in my life. Last year in Lakeland was the best year I ever had, because of Ellen and Todd, and the others. And then, all of a sudden, whoosh, I'm whizzed away from all of that, and back to trying to make friends all over again. I just don't know if I can do it.''

I noticed that tears were beginning to fill her eyes, and I realized that things weren't getting any better for her. I wanted desperately to be able to help her, but I couldn't even think of anything to say.

''I'm sorry I was so late getting home the other night,'' I said. ''I just forgot all about the time. Thanks for not telling Mom and Dad.''

''It didn't matter. I went to bed early anyway,'' she said.

I had come up here to talk about my problems, and we ended up talking about hers, but I felt better anyway. I realized that my problems weren't so bad compared to what Molly had been going through. I just wished that I could help her in some way, but it seemed to me that the only person who could help her was herself. Maybe if she had more confidence in herself she wouldn't have such a hard time making friends.

''How's the guitar going?'' I asked.

''Pretty well,'' she said.

''Can I hear something?''

She played a few songs for me, and I had to admit, she was very good. I was surprised at how quickly she was progressing. I told her I thought she sounded great, but I'm not sure she believed me.

''Did you try out for glee club yet?'' I asked.

She shook her head. ''I'm not sure if I'm going to. It seems kinds of dumb,'' she said.

''But you love to sing, and you might meet some nice people.''

''I doubt if I'd make it anyway.''

''Molly, you've got a great voice. You'll make it.

And anyway, you'll never know till you try. If you don't try you'll never get anywhere.''

"You're sounding like Mom again," she said.

"But it's true. Mom's right. You can't just sit around and expect things to happen to you. No wonder you're miserable.''

Her eyes filled with tears again.

"Oh, you don't understand any better than they do. Why don't you just get out of here and go back to brooding about your new boyfriends," she said.

"Okay, if that's what you want," I said, and I walked out of her room. If she didn't want help no one could give it to her.

It was ten o'clock. Mark still hadn't called. I still wished there was someone I could talk to about it, but I decided it was a problem I'd have to solve on my own. I would wait and see what happened this week. Maybe it would be best if I just didn't see Mark anymore. He only seemed to make me miserable most of the time. When Jimmy and I had gone out I had never felt this way. Of course, I had never really cared much about him. He never made me feel the way Mark did, as if I was very special, and very smart, and even pretty. I still couldn't figure out why someone as good-looking and together as Mark wanted to go out with me anyway. I guess that was part of the problem. I couldn't bring myself to believe he really cared about me. The phone didn't ring again that night, and once again I fell asleep trying to get Mark and Francie out of my mind.

* * * *Chapter Nine*

       Amy's parents had agreed happily to let her have the party, so Susan, Amy and I spent a good part of the next week talking about it. I was finding that the better I got to know Amy, the more I liked her. The party was going to be on Saturday. She had asked about twenty people, and most had said they could come. By Tuesday I still had not heard from Mark, nor seen him at school. I was looking forward to seeing him in our photography club meeting, but on Wednesday when I arrived at the club room there was a note on the door. Mr. Daniels was sick, and the meeting was canceled until next week. The only instructions were to continue work on our projects. I was reading the note over and trying to decide what to do when Mark came up behind me.

    "Where've you been hiding all week?" he said. "I

was beginning to think you'd moved back to Lakeland," he said. I was tempted to tell him he could have
picked up the phone if he was really worried, but I bit
my tongue.

"Nope, no such luck," I said.

"No meeting today, I see," he said, after reading
the note. "Well, what are you planning to do all
afternoon? Is there any way I could be included in your
plans?"

Suddenly I remembered that Billy had said he had a
game that afternoon. Should I mention it?

"Well, since the meeting's been canceled, I was
going to watch Billy's little league soccer game. Want
to come?"

"I'd love to."

Mark had the car, so we got our books and cameras
and walked out toward the parking lot. I wasn't entirely
sure how to get to Billy's school, which was where the
games were played, so we spent a few minutes driving
around in circles, but finally between the two of us we
figured out how to get there. Then we had to drive
around the campus looking for the right field.

"By the time we get there the game will be over," I
said.

"Maybe we can get some locker room interviews,"
said Mark.

Finally we found the right field, and Mark parked
the car. We walked over to where a few spectators,
mostly mothers, were sitting. Mom was not there,
which relieved me. I still wasn't ready for her to meet
Mark yet. When Billy saw us he waved happily from
his position as halfback. I was glad we had come.

We got out our cameras and began taking pictures.
The kids were cute and made great subjects. Billy got a

nice goal and made some good passes and kicks. I knew he'd be very proud of himself that night.

After the game, which his team won, six to four, Billy came running over to Mark and me. "Did you see me make that goal?" he asked.

"Yes. You really played well," I said.

"I'll say," said Mark. "That was a great kick you made in the last quarter, too."

We took a few more shots, some of the winners rejoicing, and some of the losers looking sad and defeated. I felt sorry for one little boy on the losing team who had missed the ball and let the goal in. He looked miserable. I shouted to Billy that I'd see him at home, and Mark and I headed for his car. On the way home we laughed and talked about the game, and about photography, and once again I felt good. I wished it could always be like this. If only there was no Francie to worry about.

When he stopped the car in front of my house, he said, "Listen, Maria's having a party this Saturday. I was wondering if you'd like to go with me?"

For a minute I was torn. I wanted to go with Mark, but I knew I had to go to Amy's party. It wouldn't be fair to back out now. Anyway, I told myself, I probably wouldn't have any fun at Maria's. I would just feel uncomfortable and immature, the way I had at Pete's Pizza.

"I'm sorry," I said. "I can't. Amy's having a party that night, too, and I've helped plan it and everything. I have to go to hers."

"Oh, I see. Well, I guess I'll see you in school then, if you don't continue to hide from me," he said.

I laughed. "I haven't been hiding from you." I almost asked him if he wanted to come to Amy's party, but I decided it would be dumb. I knew he'd much rather go to Maria's where all his friends would be. I tried not to think about the fact that Francie would be there, too.

"Thanks for coming to Billy's game," I said.

"I had a good time," he said. "And I think I got some good shots. I'll show them to you when they're done. And I want to see yours, too. They'll probably be much better than mine."

"Hah. You're the sports photographer, not me."

"We'll see."

As I got out of the car he took my hand for a minute. "See you soon," he said.

It had been a fun afternoon, and I knew that it had meant a lot to Billy that we had come.

That night at dinner Billy told everyone all about the game, and after every sentence he said, "Isn't that right, Jen?" or "Remember that, Jenny?" I was touched to see how happy I had made him just by coming to one game. That night Billy asked me to come up and say good night to him, which I often do. I read him a story, and then we talked for a while.

"Do you like it here?" he asked me.

"Most of the time I do," I said. "How about you?"

"Most of the time. But Molly doesn't. I heard her tell Todd on the phone that she hated it here."

"Well, she'll get used to it. It takes some people longer than others."

"I hope she'll get to like it soon," he said. "I don't like it when Molly's sad."

"I know," I said. "I don't either. Maybe we'll have to think of something to cheer her up."

I gave him a hug and a kiss good night, and thought about how Molly's bad moods seemed to be affecting everyone in the family.

I went back downstairs to call Amy to tell her that Mark wouldn't be coming to the party. I explained about the other party that he was already going to.

"You'll still be coming, though, won't you?" she asked quickly

"Of course. I wouldn't miss it for anything," I said.

I was glad now that I had told Mark I was going to Amy's party. She was nervous enough as it was, and it wouldn't be fair to hurt her by backing out now. I did wish Mark would be there though.

The next day at school, Susan came up to me as I was getting my things out of my locker. "It's too bad about that party that Maria's having. All the juniors will be going to that. I told Steve and Mark to come to Amy's if Maria's wasn't any fun. Mark said maybe they would."

It amused me the way Susan took it upon herself to organize Amy's party. From the way she talked anyone would have thought it was her party. Anyway, I was glad that there was a chance that Mark might come to Amy's, even though I didn't really expect him to.

At lunch, Susan, Amy, and I sat together to plan the last-minute details of the party. Amy was very nervous and I hoped for her sake that the party would be a success.

"Richard is definitely coming," she said, "and that's all I care about."

I hoped that she and Richard would have a good time together, but I had a feeling that it wasn't going to work out the way we had planned it.

I saw Richard in math class, and he asked me if I was going to the party. I said I was, and he said, "Great, can I pick you up?"

I was aghast. Apparently he had no idea that he was supposed to be Amy's date. I stuttered a bit, not knowing what to say, and he said, "Listen, if you have another date, I understand."

"Well, it's not that," I said. He was the one with another date, not me, I thought. "But I have to go early to help Amy get ready. Thanks anyway," I said quickly, and then I hurried away before he could say anything else.

I didn't have a chance to talk to Susan alone until after school. She was walking home, and I caught up to her so we could walk together.

"Richard asked me if he could pick me up for Amy's party."

"You're kidding!" she said in a horrified tone, but then Susan tends to be a bit dramatic at times. "What did you say?"

"I just said I was going over early to help get ready. I really didn't know what to say. Obviously he doesn't have any idea that he's supposed to be Amy's date."

"Richard's so out of it he wouldn't know a frog if he sat on one," she said. "Poor Amy. I wonder what we should do. She really likes Richard, but it doesn't appear to be mutual."

"Well, I don't know what we can do. I mean, we can't force him to be her date."

We had reached Susan's house, and I stopped. "Come on in," she said. We went inside, and she fixed us both a Coke, and offered me some chocolate chip cookies. "I'm glad you're not always on a diet like Amy. It's no fun. She never wants to eat anything. She does look much better since she lost all that weight, though. She only needs to lose about five more pounds, but she thinks she's still terribly overweight. I guess she can't adjust to her new body. She lost twenty-five pounds last summer, you know."

''I didn't know it was that much. I guess that's why she's so insecure about dating and boys.''

Susan nodded. ''She's never had a boyfriend, and hardly ever even had a date. Richard's the first boy who's ever paid any attention to her at all. That's why she was so excited when she thought he was going to ask her out.''

''Well, there will be lots of other guys at the party. Maybe one of them will work out better for her.''

''Yeah, maybe. I just wish she'd let Richard know he was supposed to be her date. Well, all we can do is wait and see.''

We talked for a while longer, and then I gathered up my books and walked the three doors back to my house. It was fun having a friend like Susan who lived so close by. In Lakeland we had had more land, and the houses were more spread out. Nobody my age had lived within walking distance. At first I had thought I would miss the extra space, and wouldn't like living in a neighborhood, but now I was beginning to see that it did have its good points.

When I got home, Mom was already home from work. She was puttering around the kitchen, and looking slightly frazzled.

''Did you have a hard day?'' I asked her. She nodded.

''And I forgot to leave anything out to eat tonight. It's going to be slim pickin's, I'm afraid,'' she said.

I looked in the fridge. I had to admit, there wasn't much.

''If there's a frozen pie crust I'll make a quiche.''

''That would be great, honey. Do you mind?''

''Nope. I haven't made one in a while, but I think I can remember how.''

My grandmother had taught both Molly and me how to cook when we visited her for a week last summer on the shore. It had rained the entire week, so the three of us spent the whole time in the kitchen, learning to cook and eating. It had been sort of a weird vacation, but actually it had been fun, and since Grandma had lived in France for three years, she taught us to make all sorts of great things. I've forgotten all but the easiest, like quiche, which is a cinch if you use a pie crust that's already made. Grandma would have a fit if she knew we used frozen pie crusts, but as Mom says, "What she doesn't know won't hurt her." Whenever Grandma comes to visit us Mom has to hide all the convenience foods. Grandma thinks everything should be made from scratch. Cooking is her hobby, and she's really a gourmet cook. She's even written a cookbook.

I made a quiche, and it turned out really well, if I do say so myself. Everyone had seconds, even Dad who is supposed to be watching his weight. "This is delicious, Jenny," he said. "Even Grandma would be proud."

"In spite of the frozen crust?" I asked.

"She'd never know," he said.

"What's everyone doing this weekend?" asked Mom.

"I have a game Saturday. You promised you'd come," said Billy.

"I know. We're coming," said Mom.

"Wouldn't miss it," said Dad.

"I'm going to Amy Cooke's party Saturday night," I said. "The one that Susan and I have been helping her plan. And I've got to spend some time working on my photography project."

"How about you, Molly? Any plans?" asked Dad.

Molly shrugged and rolled her eyes. "Another exciting weekend," she said.

"Well, if everyone's going to be home tomorrow, maybe we should all go to a movie," said Mom.

Molly rolled her eyes again. "What movie is there that we'd all want to see?" she asked.

Mom looked offended, but in this case I had to agree with Molly. I wasn't in the mood for a family Disney, and with Billy, there wasn't much choice.

"Well, we could look," said Mom. "There might be something we'd all enjoy."

It ended up that Mom and Dad took Billy to something that neither Molly nor I wanted to see. Molly and I stayed home and decided to bake cookies since there was nothing edible in the whole house.

"Just what I need," said Molly. "I've got to lose some weight before Todd comes."

"You don't need to lose any weight, Molly. You're just right," I said. Molly is one of those people who always thinks she has to lose five pounds, even though she's not at all fat.

While we made cookies we laughed about the vacation we had spent with Grandma when we did nothing but cook and eat.

"I wonder if we'll go to the shore again this summer," said Molly.

"Probably all of us will go," I said. "Mom and Dad will have more time for a vacation this year."

"Todd is thinking about getting a job there next summer. If he does, I'm going to, too. Do you think Mom and Dad will let me?"

"I guess so. Especially if you lived with Grandma. Do you think Todd will be able to find a job though?"

"Sure. Why not?"

I refrained from pointing out that there are usually thousands of college and high school kids looking for work on the shore in the summer, and that Todd would only be fifteen. I figured if it made her happy to think he was going to get a job there she might as well have her dream.

By the time Mom and Dad and Billy got home from the movie Molly and I had already polished off half the cookies.

"We did save a few for you guys though," said Molly.

Mom said it was past time for Billy to go to bed, but if Molly would play a few songs on the guitar for everyone, he could stay up a little while longer.

"Please," begged Billy, who would listen to a three-year-old play the violin if it meant staying up later.

"Okay" said Molly. She ran upstairs to get her guitar, and played for almost half an hour. It was amazing how much she had learned in the short time since her birthday.

* * * Chapter Ten

Saturday was overcast, but there was no sign of rain, a perfect day for taking pictures. Dad was going to the college to catch up on some work, and I asked if I could go along to take some pictures of the women athletes. He said he would be home by 4:30, which would give me plenty of time to get ready for Amy's party.

The campus is beautiful, especially in the fall. It looks exactly the way you would expect a college campus to look. The buildings are all brick and covered with ivy, and there are lots of stately old trees. I left Dad at his office and walked down to the sports fields. I had been there a few times before, so I knew my way around, more or less. There were several women running on the track. I stopped to watch for a while, and then put a telephoto lens on my camera so I wouldn't have to get too close and distract the runners. I took a roll there, and then went inside the gym. There were dancers practicing routines and doing exercises at the barre in front of a mirror. I asked them if they minded if I took some pictures. They said no, and paid no attention to me at all, which was just what I wanted. I wanted candid pictures, not anything posed and fake-looking. I got some good shots of the dancers and used almost another whole roll.

Finally I went into the swimming pool area. I had Dad's faculty pass with me, so I was allowed in. One woman was working on her time with a coach. Apparently she couldn't get it quite as fast as they wanted, because every time she stopped, the coach would shake her head and look at the stopwatch, and the swimmer would look disappointed. I tried to get some shots of the interaction between the coach and the swimmer. I got one that I thought would be great; the swimmer's arms were up on the side of the pool, folded, and the coach was squatting down talking to her. I hoped it would come out as well as I thought it might.

There were also some divers practicing compli-cated-looking twists and turns in midair. I tried to catch them in the air or just as they hit the water, but I wasn't sure how they would turn out. Shots like that require split-second timing.

When I finished my third roll I looked at the time and was amazed to see that it was already past four. I started back to Dad's office right away, hoping he wasn't already mad at me for keeping him waiting. As it turned out I needn't have worried. He was in confer-ence with a student. When he saw me at the door, he said, "Hi, Jen. I'll be a few minutes still. Why don't you go over to the cafeteria and get something to eat? Give me another half an hour."

I went to the cafeteria and got a Coke, waited for half an hour, and went back. The student was still there. It was almost five o'clock. At this rate we wouldn't be home until 5:30. I was going to have to hurry if I was going to get to Amy's by 6:30 as I had promised. I should have known better than to trust Dad when he said he'd be home by 4:30. He has no sense of time. If it weren't for Mom he'd never get anywhere on time. I still had to wash my hair and decide what to wear, which always takes forever. I hung around the hall staring at the bulletin board outside Dad's office, and finally the student left.

"Sorry, Jenny," said Dad. "He's having a hard time and I'm his advisor. I just couldn't cut him short. I'll be ready to go in just a minute."

I guess that's what makes Dad a good teacher. He really does care about his students. I wished more of my teachers felt that way. It took Dad another ten minutes of fussing around with papers before we were ready to go. Finally he got his coat and we walked out to the car.

"Did you get some good pictures?" he asked.

I told him all about what I had taken. Both Dad and Mom are very encouraging about my photography, though neither understands much about it. The only pictures they ever take are with an Instamatic or a Polaroid, and now they don't even do that because they rely on me to take all the pictures. Mom still tries occasionally because she says there won't be any pictures of me if I'm the only one who takes them.

It had started to rain as we left the building, and by the time we reached the car it was coming down hard. It took us longer than usual to get home because of the rain, so it was almost six when we finally came back. I ran upstairs to start getting ready for the party. Molly was in the bathroom. I shouted at her that I was in a hurry and that I had to take a bath.

"Just a minute," she said. "I'm washing my hair."

I went back to my room and tried to decide what to wear, but I couldn't make up my mind until after I had washed my hair and was ready to dress. I waited a few more minutes and then went and pounded on the bathroom door again.

"All right," shouted Molly. "Just a minute. You don't own the bathroom, you know."

"I'm late already. Just hurry," I yelled.

She finally emerged about five minutes later with her hair wrapped in a towel.

"Are you going out?" I asked.

"No, but you don't have to be going out to wash your hair, you know."

"I know. I was just curious. I hope you left some hot water."

I hardly had time to get the soap out of my hair before the water turned freezing. Thanks a lot, Molly, I thought. I got out of the shower, grabbed a towel and ran to my room. I reached for my hair dryer and discovered that it was missing.

"Mollyyy," I screamed. I was furious. I knew she had borrowed it. She likes mine better than her own because it dries your hair faster. I went and pounded on her locked door. "Do you have my hair dryer?" I shouted. There was no answer. Her stereo was blaring, and my hair dryer was whirring away. I pounded again and yelled some more, but she still couldn't hear me over the noise in her room. I was so mad I was about to break the door down when she finally heard me and turned off the dryer and unlocked the door.

"Calm down," she said. "You don't have to get hysterical."

"I've been pounding out here for hours," I yelled at her. "You couldn't hear me. I told you I'm late, and you knew I had to dry my hair. Why'd you take my hair dryer?"

"Oh, sorry. I thought I'd be done by the time you needed it."

"Well, thanks a lot. Now I'm going to be so late it's ridiculous, and my hair will look terrible on top of it."

"Here, take your hair dryer. Good grief. I said I was sorry."

I grabbed my hair dryer and stomped out of her room. I dried my hair, and just as I had predicted it came out looking terrible, which made me even madder. If I don't start drying my hair right away when it's wet it never turns out properly, and since I had to waste so much time trying to get the dryer from Molly it was half dry when I started. I think I mentioned that I'm very superstitious about my hair. When it turns out well, I always think it's a good sign for the night, and when it turns out badly, it's a bad sign. Well, if my theory was correct, tonight was going to be a disaster. I couldn't decide what to wear, and since I was in such a hurry I didn't have time to find just the right things. I finally settled on a pair of slacks and a blouse that I don't really like, and I felt horribly unattractive when I looked in the mirror. My hair was a mess and my clothes looked terrible, but it was past seven and there was no time to change now. Looking back on that night, I wish I had listened to my hair and stayed home.

I went downstairs in a terrible mood. Mom was in the kitchen fixing dinner.

"What was going on up there?" she asked. "It sounded like World War III."

I told Mom what Molly had done. "She's so thoughtless it's unbelievable. Now I'll be an hour late getting to Amy's, thanks to Molly," I said. "Can you give me a ride to the party?" I asked Mom. "I'll get a ride home with someone there."

"Don't you want any dinner?" she asked. "It's almost ready."

"I don't have time," I said. "There will be food at the party."

Mom dropped me at Amy's, and as I walked up to the house I tried to forget about how angry I was and get in a better mood. Susan and Amy were waiting for me. I explained why I was so late, without going into much detail. It didn't seem like the time to start complaining about family hassles.

"What needs to be done?" I asked Amy.

"Everything's all ready. All we have to do is wait for everyone to show up," she said. "I wonder who will be the first to arrive."

Soon there was a knock on the door, and Amy ran to answer it. In a few minutes more kids arrived, and soon the room was full and the music was blaring.

No one danced in the beginning, and I could tell that Amy was worried that her party was going to be a flop. Susan and Tony were the first ones to dance, and pretty soon others followed. I looked around for Richard Black, hoping he would ask Amy to dance. I saw him standing near the door, and when he saw me he waved and came over to stand beside me.

"What have you been doing all weekend?" he asked. I told him about the pictures I had taken and explained about my photography project.

"I hear you're a terrific photographer," he said.

"Well, I've got a lot to learn, but I do love it," I said.

He started asking all about the project, and about what kind of photography I liked best, and before I

knew it I was talking away without even thinking about
Amy. It happens that talking about photography is my
weakness, and I'll talk about it for hours to anyone
who'll listen. I was just about to launch into an expla-
nation of natural light photography when I looked over
and saw Amy watching us. I stopped talking, and when
I stopped, Richard said suddenly, ''Hey let's dance,
okay?''

I wasn't quite sure what to say, but I knew I couldn't
dance with him. ''I don't feel like it just yet,'' I said.
''Why don't you ask Amy? I'm sure she'd like to.''

Richard hesitated for a minute, and then he looked at
Amy and said, ''Well, okay. I'll see you later,
though.''

I could see Amy's face light up when Richard came
up to her and asked her to dance. There weren't many
extra guys there, so I didn't have much hope of anyone
else asking me to dance. Most of them were already
attached, and would probably dance with their dates all
night. I didn't care, because I didn't feel like dancing
anyway. Mark was the only person I would have
wanted to dance with. I kept thinking about the party at
Maria's. Was Francie there? I wondered. I wished now
that I had asked Mark to come to this party after all. It
was going to be a long night.

Lots of people were dancing now, and Susan came
over to me and whispered, ''Things are finally beginning to get off the ground. And I saw Richard dancing
with Amy a while ago.''

I nodded, and was just about to reply, when Richard
suddenly appeared at my elbow.

''Ready to dance yet?'' he asked.

''Well, I was just going to get something to drink,'' I
said.

''Okay. This time I promise I won't spray it all over

you.'' He got two Cokes and handed one to me. I looked around the room for Amy, and saw her dancing with a tall thin boy whose name I didn't know. I asked Richard who he was.

"That's Sam Whittier. He's in my English class. Also Amy's English class. They're both literature freaks. I think Sam has a bit of a crush on Amy. I hope it's mutual."

Well, I thought. This is interesting. I guess there's no hope for Amy and Richard. I knew that Susan would be upset, but Amy looked happy dancing with Sam. They danced a few more times and then came over to where I was standing. While Sam poured them some drinks I whispered to Amy, "Are you having a good time?"

She nodded. "Sam asked me to the football game tomorrow."

"That's great," I said.

"He's so nice, and I feel as though I can really relax with him. I don't think it would ever have worked out between Richard and me."

Hooray. At least I didn't have to worry about Amy anymore. When Richard asked me to dance again, I said yes. We danced for a while, and then went outside to get some air. I guess I should have known better, but it didn't occur to me that Richard liked me as anything more than a friend. It was a beautiful night, clear and cool. The moon was so bright we could see as clearly as if it had been daylight. I sat down on the front steps, glad to be outside for a few minutes. Richard sat down beside me. "It's nice out here," I said.

"It is," he said. "Umm, Jenny . . ." he began, and then, all of a sudden he was kissing me. I was so shocked I didn't know what to do, and for a minute I didn't do anything. Then I stopped and said, "Wait a minute, Richard, I think we'd better talk.''

I looked up, and just at that moment I saw Steve and Julie, followed by Mark, coming up the driveway just a few feet away. Mark stopped as soon as he saw me, and I could tell by the expression on his face that he had seen Richard kiss me.

''Well, hi,'' he said. ''Looks like a good party. No wonder you didn't ask me to come the other day. I was just dropping Steve and Julie off. See you later.''

Before I could say a word he was gone. I heard the Volkswagen start up and speed off.

''Oh, God,'' I said. ''I knew this night was going to be a disaster.''

Then Richard said, ''I think I'm beginning to get the picture. You and Mark have a thing going, don't you?''

''Well, we did. Now I'm not so sure,'' I said.

''I'm really sorry, Jenny. I didn't know. I thought maybe . . .'' He didn't finish his sentence, but I knew what he meant.

''It's not your fault. I guess I've just been so wrapped up in trying to figure Mark out that I didn't think about anyone else. If I've led you on, I'm sorry. I didn't mean it. I thought we were just friends.''

''You never gave me any reason to think we were anything more than friends,'' he said. ''I guess it was just wishful thinking. Can we still be friends?''

I nodded. ''I hope so. I don't want to lose all my friends tonight.''

''I'm really sorry about Mark,'' Richard said again. ''If you want I'll talk to him and explain what happened.''

I shook my head. ''Thanks, but I think I'd better explain this one myself.''

* * * *Chapter Eleven*

    The following week was the longest of my life. I kept hoping I would run into Mark so that I could explain what had happened, but he was nowhere to be seen. I thought about calling him, but I wasn't sure how he would react, and I wanted to explain what had happened in person. On Tuesday after classes I waited for him near his car, but when I saw him walking toward the parking lot with Francie I slid between some cars and ran out the side entrance of the lot before they saw me. How could I talk to him with Francie standing there and flipping her blond hair around like she was some kind of model?

    When he didn't show up for the photography meeting the next day I realized that he was avoiding me on purpose. I was miserable all through the meeting. I had to talk to him, but it was beginning to look as though I wouldn't ever get a chance. He meant too much to me to let our relationship be ruined by a foolish misunderstanding. Finally I decided to write him a note asking him to give me a chance to explain what he had seen. Once I had made that decision I felt better. At least I was taking a positive action rather than just waiting to run into him.

At the end of the meeting Mr. Daniels said, "I have some exciting news. We've been invited to participate in the New England Photography Conference, which will take place at the White Top Mountain Winter Resort, on the weekend before Thanksgiving. I know this is short notice as that's only ten days away, but there were some openings left, and the conference committee asked me if I had any students who would like to attend. There will be speakers, displays, and a field demonstration of natural photography techniques. The price is fifty dollars, but that includes all meals and the price of a bed. We'll go up Saturday morning and come back Sunday night. We'll drive up in my van if we can all fit. I think you'll find it worthwhile, and a lot of fun as well. Anyone who's interested please see me after the meeting."

It sounded terrific. After the meeting I went up to Mr. Daniels and told him I wanted to go, but I had to check with my parents. I prayed that Mom and Dad would let me go. Fifty dollars was a lot, but I hoped I could convince them that it would be worth it.

As I walked home that afternoon I thought about what I should say in my note to Mark. I finally decided I would just say, "Please let me explain what happened the other night. Can we talk?" I went home and wrote the note and put it in a sealed envelope. Then I took it over to Susan and Steve's house. Steve and Mark had several classes together, so I asked him to give it to

Mark the next day. I could tell that Susan was dying of curiosity, but I didn't feel like telling her all about my problems. I told her I had mountains of homework and went on home.

That night at dinner both Mom and Dad seemed to be in good moods so I decided it was a good time to ask them about the conference. "Guess what," I said. "Mr. Daniels announced that our photography club has been invited to participate in the New England Photography Conference."

"That sounds interesting," said Dad. "When is it?"

"The weekend before Thanksgiving. It's going to be held at White Top Mountain."

"White Top Mountain. That's quite a ways from here, isn't it?" asked Mom.

"Three hours. But Mr. Daniels said he'd drive us up there. And it's going to be great. They've got all sorts of well-known speakers, and displays, and workshops and everything. Can I go? I know it'll be worth it."

"It sounds great, honey. I don't see any reason why you shouldn't go if your teacher's going to be driving you all up there," said Mom.

"Well, there's just one little thing," I said. "It costs fifty dollars."

"I'd say that's fifty little things," said Dad. "And that sounds like a lot for a two-day conference."

"But that includes meals and lodging for the night," I said. "And Mr. Daniels said it will be a good experience for us. I think I'd really learn a lot if I went."

"Well, I'll tell you what," said Dad. "We'll pay for half, and you can pay the rest out of your baby-sitting money. We'll lend you all the money now, and you can pay us back twenty-five dollars as you earn it. Does that sound fair?" he asked.

It was going to take a lot of baby-sitting to earn twenty-five dollars, plus what I would need for Christmas, but it would be worth it. I nodded. "Thanks, Dad," I said.

"Well, you can start earning right away," said Mom. "We have to go out both Friday and Saturday nights this weekend, and Molly is baby-sitting for the Wilcoxes. Do you want to sit for Billy?"

"Okay," I said. It wouldn't be a very exciting weekend, but I needed the money. Besides, I didn't have any plans, and the way things were between Mark and me, it didn't look as if anything was going to come up.

The following day I spent every minute wondering if Mark had gotten my note. When I still hadn't seen or heard from him by that afternoon, I began to wonder if Steve had forgotten to give it to him. On my way home I stopped at the Jennings house. Susan was the only one home. We talked for a while, and I was just about to leave when Steve finally came in. He didn't mention the note, and I didn't want to seem overanxious by asking him, but finally I couldn't stand the suspense any longer.

"Did you see Mark today?" I asked him.

"Oh, yeah," he said. "I almost forgot to give him your note, but I remembered it just as I was about to leave. Luckily he was still there."

"So you gave it to him?"

"Yup."

"Thanks, Steve."

"Anytime."

He hadn't gotten the note until this afternoon, but at least he had gotten it. Maybe he would call tonight, I thought. I went right home in case he was trying to get hold of me.

He didn't call, but the next morning when I got to school, Mark was waiting by my locker. My heart started beating a mile a minute when I saw him. I had rehearsed what I was going to say to him a thousand times in my head, but now that I finally had the chance to explain I could hardly get the words out.

"Hi. I got your note," he said when I got to my locker. His voice sounded formal and cold.

"Good. Listen, about the other night. I know how it must have looked, but Richard and I are just friends."

"Very good friends, I guess. Do you treat all your friends that way?"

"Look, Richard misunderstood. He thought there was more to it, and he kissed me. I was so startled I didn't do anything for a minute, and that's what you happened to see. It was just a misunderstanding. He's in my math class and he's helped me out with some work. I danced with him at Amy's, but until he kissed me I had no idea how he felt. As soon as he understood that I didn't feel the same way, he apologized, and we're still friends, but nothing more."

"But why didn't you ask me to go to Amy's party with you? I know Amy told you you could invite me, because Susan told Steve we were invited."

"When you said you were going to Maria's I just figured you'd rather be there. I mean, all your friends were there and everything," I said.

"All my friends except the one who counts," he said, and he took my hand. "Don't you know I'd rather be with you than anyone else?"

"Once I was at Amy's I wished I had asked you. I had a miserable time. And all week I've wanted to see you to clear this up. On Tuesday I even waited for you by your car, but you were with Francie, so I didn't want to bother you, and then when you weren't at the photography club meeting I was desperate, so I wrote you the note.''

"Well, I'm glad you did. I've been miserable all week, too. Listen, I'm late for class right now. Are you busy tonight? Do you want to go out with me?'' he asked.

"I'd love to,'' I said. I was so happy that things were okay between us that I almost forgot that I had promised Mom I'd baby-sit. "Oh, wait a minute,'' I cried. "I promised Mom I'd sit for Billy both nights this weekend.''

Mark looked disappointed. "Both nights?'' he said.

"Look, maybe you could come over to my house,'' I said.

"Would your parents let me if you're supposed to be sitting?'' he asked.

"I don't know, but they don't have to find out. Come over at about eight o'clock tonight.''

"Okay. See you tonight.'' He gave my hand a squeeze and we both hurried to class.

I floated through the morning in a cloud of happiness. I was so relieved that Mark understood what had happened. I thought about what he had said. "Don't you know I'd rather be with you than anyone else?'' I wasn't even worried about Francie anymore. He had made it clear that I was the one he really cared about.

After math class Richard came over to my desk. I hadn't seen him to talk to since the night at Amy's.

"How's it going?'' he asked. "Did you do all right on the quiz?''

"Yes, I passed, thanks to your help. I'm beginning to get confused again though. My mind hasn't been on my work lately. I've got to start paying closer attention.''

"Still worried about Mark?'' he asked.

"Well, we talked and got it worked out, so things are pretty good between us now," I said.

"That's great," he said. "Well, see you later."

That afternoon I walked home with Susan. "Did you hear that Amy's going out with Sam again tomorrow?" she said.

"No, that's great. Looks like those two are an item," I said. I was happy for Amy.

"How are things going with you and Mark?" she asked.

"Fine, now," I said. "We had a misunderstanding, but we talked it out this morning. He's coming over tonight. Are you going out with Tony this weekend?"

"We're going to the movies tonight. Why don't you and Mark come too?"

"That would be fun, but I have to baby-sit for Billy, so we have to stay home."

"You're lucky your parents let Mark come over when you're baby-sitting," she said.

"Well, they don't exactly know he's coming," I said.

"Oh, I get it. Well, don't worry. I won't say anything."

We had reached her house and she turned up her drive.

"See you later. Have fun tonight," I said.

I felt guilty about having Mark come over without asking Mom and Dad. I thought about telling them, and explaining how important it was that I see him, but what if they said he couldn't come. I decided I couldn't take the chance. I just wouldn't tell them, and they'd never find out.

Mom and Dad were going out for dinner and then to a play, so they wouldn't be home until eleven at the earliest. Molly was baby-sitting, so Billy and I had

dinner alone together. I fixed hot dogs and Spaghet-
tios, his favorites, and even made homemade brownies
for dessert. Just after I'd given him his brownie I said,
"Listen, Billy. Mark's coming over for a while tonight, okay?"

"Sure. I like him. He's much better than that creepy
Jimmy you went out with in Lakeland. Do you think
he'd like to see my collection of monster cards?"

"I don't know. He might," I said. Anything to keep
him quiet.

"Listen, I'd rather you didn't say anything to Mom
and Dad about him coming over, okay."

"Okay. Why?"

"Well, they might think I shouldn't have guests
when I'm supposed to be watching you, but I know
you're big enough that you don't need watching all the
time. So let's just keep it a secret, okay?"

"Okay. She said you could have Susan over
though."

"Yeah, but that's sort of different," I said, praying
he wouldn't ask why. "Listen, if you keep it a secret,
Mark and I will come to another game really soon,
okay? Want another brownie?"

"Okay."

Now all I had to do was hope he remembered and
didn't say something stupid by mistake.

At a few minutes past eight the doorbell rang, and
there was Mark. I was so happy to see him that I forgot
to be worried or feel guilty. "Come on in," I said.
"Everyone's out but Billy, and I bribed him to keep his
mouth shut with brownies and a promise to come to
another game. You may have to pretend to be en-
thralled by his monster cards, though."

"Do you think your parents would be upset if they
knew I was here?" he asked.

"You don't know Mom and Dad. They're okay, but when it comes to something like this, they might not like it."

Mark was wearing a yellow sweater that looked great with his dark eyes, and jeans, and when he smiled I was so happy that he had come, and that everything was good between us. I got us some Cokes and we sat in the living room on the couch. As soon as Billy heard that Mark was here he ran downstairs, dragging his whole collection of monster cards. Mark was forced to rave over every one.

Fortunately the Hulk was on at 8:30, so Billy's presentation was cut short, and Mark and I were able to have some privacy. He had brought the pictures that he had taken at Billy's game. They were fantastic. I was embarrassed to tell him that I hadn't even developed mine yet. There was one of Billy that was particularly good. "I love this one," I said. "It really catches something about Billy. He's so sure of himself, but so vulnerable at the same time."

"Like you," said Mark.

"Me, sure of myself, ha."

"You come off that way, even if you aren't." As he said it he looked right at me, staring hard. "You should be sure of yourself, with your looks."

Before I could say anything he kissed me, a long perfect kiss. He put his arms around me and we kissed again, and I forgot everything else. I wasn't even worried about Billy barging in.

"I've been wanting to do that forever. I missed you so much this week," he said.

"Me, too. Next time we have a misunderstanding, let's talk about it right away. I couldn't stand another week like the past one."

"I promise," he said, putting his arms around me

again. This time I pulled away, suddenly afraid that Mom and Dad were going to come in any minute.

"What's wrong?" he asked.

"I'm just worried that someone might come in, or that Mom and Dad might come home," I said.

"Don't worry," he said. He pulled me to him and kissed me again. This time I didn't resist. In a few minutes I heard Billy yelling from the kitchen. I jumped away from Mark so fast I upset my Coke. I ran to the kitchen to get a sponge to clean it up, and Mark followed me.

"Can you make popcorn?" asked Billy. "Mom said it was okay."

I looked at Mark. "Want some popcorn?"

"Sure," he said, but I could tell he'd rather have stayed in the living room. I didn't want Billy to make a fuss though, so I started making the popcorn.

"I'll be in the den watching the Hulk," said Billy. "It's really a good one."

"It's not easy finding time to be alone with you, you know that," said Mark. "Wherever we go it seems like there are always hordes of people around."

"One seven-year-old hardly constitutes a horde," I said.

"He might as well be though."

"I thought you liked doing things with your friends, like the night we went to the movies."

"Well, sometimes it's fun that way," he said.

"How's Francie, by the way?" I asked, trying to make my voice sound calm and casually interested. I figured this was a good way to find out what was going on between them.

He looked at me, surprised. "She's fine, why?"

"I just wondered. You two seem like such good friends and all."

"We are good friends. But that's all. Does it bother you?"

"No, as long as you're just friends, why should it?" I said.

"It shouldn't. And I promise you, it could never be anything else but friends between Francie and me again. Okay?"

I felt better knowing that, but somehow I still had trouble believing it. There was something about the way he looked at her. I decided not to worry about it.

I finished the popcorn and took it out to Billy. Mark and I went back into the living room. It was almost ten, so I figured we had a good half hour before he would have to leave. As soon as we had sat down on the couch, though, the door opened, and Molly came in.

"Hi, I'm home," she shouted. "Who's car is that?"

"Mine," said Mark, standing up as soon as she came into the living room. "I'm Mark Watson. You must be Molly." He held out his hand and Molly took it, staring at him with a surprised look. She glanced at me. "Does Mom know he's here?" she asked.

I shook my head. "Don't say anything, okay?"

"I won't," she said. "But what about Billy? Do you really think he'll keep his mouth shut?"

"We bribed him with brownies, popcorn, and a trip to his next game. He'd better."

"I guess I'd better be going, anyway," said Mark.

"Don't leave on my account," said Molly. "Nice to meet you," and she went out of the room and up the stairs before he could say anything more.

"I guess I should go," he said to me once we were alone again.

"I guess so. They might be home early for some reason."

Now that Molly had come home I was worried. I

wasn't sure she'd keep quiet, and I was beginning to feel guilty for not telling Mom. Mark could see that I was nervous and uncomfortable, so he kissed me quickly and said, "I'll call you tomorrow. Thanks for letting me come over."

I watched him as he ran down the steps and up the walk to his car. I was glad he had come, even if it did get me in trouble.

* * * *Chapter Twelve*

Mark had darkroom time on the following Tuesday afternoon, and he asked me if I wanted to share it with him. Since it's so hard to get time in the darkroom, I was thrilled. I still hadn't had a chance to develop the rolls I had taken the day I went to the college with Dad, so I wanted to get them done. It was fun working together.

"You know, we should always share our darkroom time. It's almost like getting twice as much that way," said Mark.

"I think it's a great idea," I said. Not only did it give me more time in the darkroom, but it gave me more time to be with Mark. Since we had cleared up our misunderstanding, things were better than ever between us. I was very happy, especially when I was with him.

On Wednesday Mark and I went to the photography club meeting. The conference was the following weekend, and those of us who were going were very excited. There were three other kids going besides Mark and me: one boy who was a senior, and a girl and another boy who were both juniors. The meeting was a short one, and when it was over Mark and I decided we had time to go to Billy's game. We had promised him we'd come again, and this seemed like a good time to do it. Mark had the car so he drove us over to Billy's school. As he was parking I noticed Mom's car parked a few spaces away.

"Oh, no," I said.

"What's wrong?" asked Mark.

"That's our car. Mom must be here."

"Well, what's so awful about that? I thought you got along well with your parents."

"Well, I do, but I just didn't want you to have to meet her today."

"Ah ha. You're afraid I'll do something horribly rude and embarrass you in front of your mother, aren't you?"

"No, just the opposite. I'm afraid she'll say something incredibly dumb and embarrass me in front of you."

"Don't worry. I won't hold you responsible for what your mother says."

"You mean, I'm not my mother's keeper!"

"Hmmm, something like that." He laughed. "Anyway, I've been wanting to meet your parents."

We walked toward the field and I looked for Mom in the group of parents sitting in the bleachers beside the field. She was sitting with one other mother, watching Billy as he ran down the field. She had on jeans and a bright green blazer, and she looked young and pretty as she laughed at something the other mother said to her.

"There she is," I said, pointing her out to Mark. "The one in the green blazer."

"She's pretty," he said. "I can see the resemblance even from here."

When we got closer I waved and shouted up to her. She looked around and when she saw me she shouted, "Hi. Come on up."

We went up the bleachers to where she was sitting. When I got there I gave her a kiss. "Hi, Mom. How's the game?"

I sat down next to her and motioned for Mark to sit next to me. "Mom, this is a friend of mine, Mark Watson. He's a photographer, too."

"Hi, Mark. It's nice to meet you. You're so nice to come to Billy's game. He'll be so excited. He loves having a cheering section."

"He's a cute kid," said Mark. "And I got some great shots last time we came."

"I just got here a few minutes ago myself," said Mom. "I'm not even sure what the score is, but I know we're winning."

"Has Billy been playing well?" I asked.

"They just put him in. Mr. Thomas is such a nice coach. I think when he sees someone's mother come he puts the kids in. That's the way it should be at this age. Do you play any sports, Mark?" she asked.

"Well, I do the sports photography for the school newspaper, so I don't have time to play any team sports this year, but I love tennis, and I love to ski."

"I guess the ski season will be starting pretty soon. Being from Ohio we've never done much skiing. Are you going on this conference that Jenny's so excited about?" she asked.

"Yes, I am. I'm looking forward to it, too. Our

photography club advisor thinks it'll be a great experience.''

"Not to mention a lot of fun, right?'' said Mom, giving me a look that said no wonder you were so keen on going. I hadn't mentioned that Mark was going too. I prayed she wouldn't say anything. I told her about the pictures Mark had taken at the last game, especially the ones of Billy.

"I'd love to see them,'' she said.

"They're in the car. I could show them to you after the game if you'd like . . .'' he said.

"Why don't you come back to the house after the game?'' I said.

"Okay.''

We watched the rest of the game which Billy's team lost in the last few minutes. Billy and his friends were very disappointed, but Billy was glad that we had come. When it was over, Mark and I went home in his car, and Mom waited to drive Billy home. When we were all back at the house we showed them the pictures.

"This is great. You've really caught Billy. Could I have a copy of this?'' Mom asked Mark.

"Sure. I'd give you this one, but I think I can make a better print and crop out some of this background,'' said Mark.

"I don't want you to go to any trouble, but that would be lovely, if you don't mind.''

"I'd love to do it.''

Mom and Mark seemed to be getting along well, which was nice. I don't know why I had been so nervous about Mark meeting them, except that I wanted them all to get along.

After a while Mark said he had to go, and we said

good-bye. When he was gone, Mom said, "I like your friend very much. He's a nice young man."

"Thanks. I like him a lot, too."

She nodded. "It shows." She smiled. "I'm happy for you."

That's all she said, but at dinner Billy told Dad about the game, and that Mark and I had come. Dad asked about Mark, and Mom said he was very nice, and told Dad about the picture.

"So, he's a photographer too? Would he by any chance be going on this conference that's putting us in the poorhouse?"

"Yes, he is going, but that's not the only reason I want to go," I said.

"Well, make sure you pay attention to more than Mark when you're up there. I suppose there will be teachers going to chaperone?"

"Yes, Dad. Don't worry."

"Actually, Mark seems very serious about his photography," said Mom. "And Jenny's latest pictures are really excellent, so I think it will be worthwhile. Look at it as an investment, dear. If Jenny becomes a successful photographer, she can support us in our old age."

Dad laughed and didn't say anything more about the conference. I gave Mom a grateful look.

I was so excited about going, and of course the next two days crawled by. Every class seemed to take a year, and I was convinced that all my teachers were conspiring to be as boring as possible. Nobody could be that dull unless they were trying. Finally Friday afternoon came. Mark dropped me off at home and said that he would pick me up in the morning. We were all to meet in the parking lot at school. It would take three hours to drive up there. The conference started at 9:30, so we wanted to leave by 6:00 A.M. Friday night I planned to pack and go to bed early.

It took me hours to decide what to take. I figured it would be very cold, and there would probably even be some snow on the ground, so I wanted to take plenty of warm clothes. I packed some hiking boots and my down parka. I also packed a skirt in case we had to dress up Saturday night, and an extra pair of jeans. I decided I'd wear my favorite jeans and a new sweater. I set my alarm for 5:00 A.M., and went to bed early.

When the alarm rang I almost turned it off and went back to sleep, but then I remembered that it wasn't just an ordinary school day, and I was wide awake. I got up, dressed warmly and went downstairs and had some toast and coffee, and waited for Mark. He came at 5:45, just as we had agreed. He had a big box of donuts for everyone to eat on the way up.

Once we were all assembled at the parking lot we piled into Mr. Daniels' van. There were no seats in the back, just a carpeted floor. He used it for camping, so there was also an ice box. We ate Mark's donuts, and talked about photography and school on the way up. The drive passed quickly.

When we got there we were given our room assignments. They were double rooms, so Sharon, the other girl, and I shared one room, Mark and David, and Mr. Daniels and Tom, the senior, were in the other two. Our room was on the second floor in the women's wing. Sharon and I went up to drop our stuff and look over the room. It was super. Very rustic with pine shingles and beams, and our own little sink. We shared a bathroom with the rest of the floor. There were four rooms on each floor.

After we registered and got our name tags we all went into the main hall for the opening talks. There was an introduction by the head of the Connecticut Photography Society, and then the opening address by a well-known nature photographer.

After the opening talks we went to different groups, depending upon what we had signed up for. I was taking Still Photography Outdoors, and Mark was taking Photographing Wildlife.

"I'll meet you at lunch," he said.

"Okay. See you later."

Sharon was in my group, so the two of us found seats together. The speaker talked for a while about still photography methods, showed some slides, discussed the use of filters, and other equipment. For the second hour we analyzed slides taken by famous still photographers. When the two hours were up I couldn't believe it. The time had flown by.

Mark and I ate with the others at a big table. Everyone seemed to have enjoyed the group they had been in. After lunch there were panel discussions by various photographers, and then some free time when we were supposed to try out some of the techniques we had talked about. Right before dinner we met back with the instructors to ask questions.

That night after dinner there was a slide show, and then an open house in which the equipment manufacturers displayed new cameras and equipment. They were also for sale. Even though it would be years before I could afford anything, it was fascinating. I especially liked looking at the darkroom equipment, as I hoped someday to have my own darkroom. Mark fell in love with a camera specially made for stop action, perfect for a sports photographer.

"It's nice to dream, isn't it?" he said.

"Yeah. Someday," I said.

We watched some of the older photographers buying equipment. Quite a few did, since everything was discounted. Mr. Daniels bought a new filter, and said he was tempted by a close-up lens, but decided he couldn't afford it. Mark bought a roll of ultraviolet film. "I've never tried this and I've always wanted to," he said.

After the equipment show Mark and I walked through the display area. There were slides going continuously, and photographs mounted on every spare inch of wall space.

"Hey, look at this," Mark called to me.

There was a group of three seascapes with the name William P. Daniels underneath. "That's Mr. Daniels," he said.

"Wow. These are great," I said. "I didn't know he was exhibiting anything, did you?"

"Not here, but I've seen his stuff on display other places. He's good. We're lucky to have him as a teacher."

The exhibit hall closed at 11:00, and Mr. Daniels found us and suggested that we all head back to the dorm and get to bed. I had to admit I was tired after getting up so early. We all started back, and Mark and I fell behind the others a little.

"Let's take a walk before breakfast, tomorrow, okay?" he said.

"Okay. What time shall we meet?"

"Well, breakfast is at eight, so how about seven-thirty. Is that okay?"

"Yes, but don't expect much in the way of conversation. I'm not at my best at seven-thirty in the morning," I said.

"You don't even have to say hello. Just meet me right here. I guarantee you'll like it once we get out in the fresh morning air," said Mark.

"Okay. See you in the morning," I said.

He kissed me good night and said, "Remember. Seven-thirty."

"I'll remember."

"Good night," I said. I went up the stairs to our room, thinking more about Mark than about photography, but when I got there Sharon was full of talk about the conference. I got ready for bed and we talked until we both fell asleep.

The next morning we woke to the alarm at seven. I got dressed, put a new roll of film in my camera, and went downstairs to meet Mark. He was already down in the lobby, talking to a man who had been in his seminar.

It was a beautiful crisp morning, and I had worn my parka and a stocking cap.

"You look like you're ready to go skiing," said Mark.

"Well, it's cold. What am I supposed to wear?" I asked.

"I'm going to teach you to ski this winter," he said. "You'll love it. Besides, you look great in a parka."

"I do want to learn, but I'm such a klutz. You'll be embarrassed to be seen with me," I said.

"With a teacher like me you'll be an expert in no time."

"Or a cripple," I said.

"Watch out." He laughed. "Comments like that will get you nowhere."

We had walked up a path that led to a view of the entire valley. It was breathtakingly beautiful. There were other photographers all around looking and tak-

ing pictures. Mark found a little path that seemed to
lead straight up.

"Come on," he said. I followed him, and after we
had climbed for a few minutes we stopped. There was
no one in sight.

"I figured we might get some privacy up here. No
one else looked ready to start climbing before breakfast. Sit down for a minute," he said.

I sat down beside him and he put his arm around me
and kissed me. It was beautiful, with a view of the
mountains and valleys that seemed to stretch on
forever. I felt as if I could have stayed there forever,
but all of a sudden we heard someone coming. We
jumped apart just as three photographers came up the
path. I suppose it was pretty obvious what we had been
doing, but they didn't pay any attention to us. Mark
looked at his watch. "It's five past eight," he said.
"We'd better go or we'll miss breakfast."

It was almost 8:30 by the time we got down to the
dining room.

"Well, where have you two been? Or shouldn't I
ask?" said David, the guy who was sharing Mark's
room.

I blushed, of course, and Mark said, "Just getting
shots of the view. It's gorgeous.

"Get some breakfast before it's all gone," said Mr.
Daniels. After breakfast we broke up right away into
small groups. The lectures that day were all geared to
darkroom work, an area that I find less exciting but
more difficult than taking the pictures. I learned a lot
that day, and by the time the conference ended at four I
felt I had gotten more than my money's worth. Dad
would be happy, I thought.

I think everyone felt it had been worthwhile, and the

drive home was fun. We were all friends by that time, and Mr. Daniels was very relaxed with us, treating us like friends rather than students. We stopped at McDonald's for dinner which we ate on the road, making a mess of Mr. Daniels' van. We all laughed a lot, and I felt that I had made some new friends. Mark drove me home after we had said good-bye to everyone. We were both tired but very happy.

"I can't believe that Thanksgiving is this Thursday already. This fall has gone so fast. Are you going to be here for Thanksgiving?" Mark asked.

"Yes, are you?" I asked.

"Yes. Let's plan to spend the day together on Friday. I know a pond where we might be able to ice skate, if you'd like."

"I'd like that," I said.

We had reached my house and were sitting in the car in front of it. I saw Mom peer out from behind the curtain. I had told her I would be home by seven, and it was almost eight, so they were probably wondering where I was.

"I'd better go in now," I said. "Thanks for the ride. It was a fun weekend."

"It was. I'll call you this week if I don't see you in school. Don't forget to save Friday."

I got out and ran up to the house. Everyone was waiting to hear all about it, and I told them everything, except, of course, that things between Mark and me were better than ever. I went to bed very tired but very happy that night.

* * * Chapter Thirteen

Everything was great until the following Tuesday, and then things began to go downhill fast. When I got home from school Tuesday afternoon, Mom met me at the door waving the phone bill.

"Do you know anything about this?" she asked.

"What do you mean?" I asked, although I knew right away what she meant. Molly had been calling Todd and her other friends in Lakeland regularly, and Mom and Dad had no idea.

"Our phone bill is fifty dollars higher than it usually is. Someone's been calling Lakeland a lot. You know how your father and I feel about long-distance calls. We can't afford bills like these. We have friends we'd like to talk to in Lakeland, too, but stamps are a lot cheaper than phone calls."

"Wait a minute, Mom. Before you start lecturing, it wasn't me. I promise not one of those is mine. Molly made every one of those calls. They're mostly to Todd, I think."

Just at that moment Molly appeared. "Thanks a lot, Jenny," she said. "I'm glad to know I can count on you to stick it to me."

"Sorry, Molly. I didn't want to tell on you, but they had to know. They'd find out as soon as they saw whose number this is."

"Jenny's right, Molly. If you made these calls you're in serious trouble, and Dad and I might as well know now."

"I'll pay for them myself," she said.

"Well, it's certainly nice to know that someone around here is rich. Just exactly where do you expect to get all this money from. There are over fifty dollars worth of bills here."

"How about baby-sitting?" she said. "And when I do it, I won't be inviting my boyfriend over the minute you go out like some people I know."

"Just what exactly do you mean by that?" asked Mom.

"Ask Jenny. I'm not a tattletale like some people, either."

Mom looked at me. "I have a feeling you'd better tell me what she's talking about."

"Well, Mark stopped by the other night when I was sitting for Billy. That's all. It wasn't any big deal," I said.

"How long was he here?" asked Mom.

"I guess about an hour or two."

"Jenny, you know perfectly well Dad and I wouldn't have allowed Mark to be here when we're out. Especially when you're supposed to be taking care of your little brother.''

I didn't say anything. I was so mad at Molly I could hardly speak.

''I think you both had better go to your rooms. When your father comes home we've got some talking to do.''

On the way upstairs I said to Molly, ''Thanks a lot. You didn't have to tell her. The only reason I told her about the phone bills was because I knew she'd find out anyway.''

Molly didn't say anything and I stomped into my room, furious.

When Dad got home Mom showed him the phone bill and I could hear his yell all the way upstairs.

''Molly, come down here please,'' he shouted.

I didn't hear what they said, but I heard Molly run back upstairs in tears a few minutes later. Then it was my turn. Mom called me and asked me to come down. ''Please tell me exactly what happened the other night,'' she said. ''The truth.''

''Mark asked if he could come over, since I had to baby-sit and couldn't go out. We really needed to talk, so I said okay. I guess I knew you would say no, so I didn't ask you.''

''And did you tell Molly and Billy not to tell us he'd been here?''

I nodded. ''I'm sorry. I know I should have told him not to come, but I had to talk to him.''

''Jenny, what upsets me is not so much that Mark was here, but that you deliberately disobeyed, and then asked Molly and Billy to help you cover it up.''

''I know. I felt terrible doing it, but I really wanted to see him.''

"Well, I just wish you'd asked us. We might have allowed him to come over for a few minutes if it was that important. I know you and Mark are serious, and I think you both can be trusted. We wouldn't have allowed it last year in Lakeland, but you are older now, and Mark is certainly more mature than Jimmy. Your father and I can be reasonable, you know. When something like this comes up again, please talk to us about it before you do something behind our backs."

"I will. I'm sorry, Mom."

"Now," said Mom, "about Molly. I think you should know that we told her Todd could not come for the weekend. I don't think he was really planning on it anyway, but she's very upset. I think it's time she forgets about Todd and starts making some new friends. I thought she was doing fine until I got this phone bill. I had no idea she'd been calling him all the time like that. How long has this been going on?"

"I don't know. The only thing I knew was that she had been calling him. I didn't want to tell you because I didn't want to be a tattletale, and I figured it was between you and her."

Mom was sitting at the kitchen table staring at the phone bill, and Dad was pacing around the kitchen not saying anything. Finally he went to the freezer and got some ice to make himself a drink.

"Want one?" he asked Mom. She nodded. They usually don't drink except on weekends, so I knew they were both upset.

As if she could read my mind, Mom said, "It's not the money that upsets us, though that's part of it, of course, but the fact that Molly felt she had to make all those calls. It's clear that she hasn't adjusted to Stromley at all. I'm very worried about her. Jenny, I know it's hard, but I wish you'd make a real effort to talk to her and spend some time with her over the next few weeks. She's furious at us for saying that Todd can't come, and I don't want her to feel that we've all forsaken her.''

Unfortunately, it was the wrong time to ask me to be nice to Molly. My sympathy for her had just about run out. I had tried before, but our relationship lately seemed to be deteriorating. I was so mad at her for telling Mom about Mark that I couldn't imagine making up right then.

''I don't think I can do much good. We haven't been getting along too well lately,'' was all I said.

Mom looked more upset than ever. She sipped her drink slowly and sighed. ''Just give it a try, okay?''

''Okay,'' I said, just because I wanted Mom to feel better, but I knew I wouldn't. As far as I was concerned, Molly was on her own. I was tired of nursemaiding her through her problems. After all, they were problems that everyone has, but most of us are able to cope with them.

Molly didn't come downstairs for the rest of the night. At dinner Billy said, ''Where's Molly?''

''She's in her room. She's upset,'' said Mom.

Billy didn't say anything more. It was a quiet meal. After dinner I knew I should knock on her door and try to talk to her, but I didn't want to. I figured she probably wouldn't answer anyway.

The next day was a short day. Classes ended at noon because of the Thanksgiving break, but Mr. Daniels had asked anyone who wanted to hear about the conference to come to a meeting right after classes. We had decided to make it into a party, and everyone brought something. I brought some cookies, and there was potato salad and ham and cheese and fruit and all sorts of cookies and brownies. Almost everyone in the club was there. We talked informally about the conference. I wasn't nervous at all because it wasn't like giving a speech or anything. I sat with Mark, Sharon, and David, and I felt really close to all of them. I was so glad I had photography and the club. It was almost three when the party finally ended.

I had the darkroom from three to five, and I asked Mark if he wanted to stay and share it with me.

"Sorry, I can't today. I've got to get home. I wish I could because I want to develop the pictures from the conference. Have you done yours yet?" he asked.

"No, that's what I'm going to do today. I can't wait to see them. Listen, can I talk to you for a minute before you go?"

"Sure, walk back to the room with me while I get my stuff," he said. I wanted to tell him about my fight with Molly, and about Mom finding out he had come over the other night. After I had told him all about it, he said, "Your parents were really upset, huh?"

"Well, more because I snuck behind their back than anything else. Actually they were pretty nice about it. I got off easy because they were so upset about Molly. I'm so mad at her for telling."

"You're lucky, you know that. I mean having parents who really care," he said.

Mark's parents were divorced. He had mentioned this several times, but he never seemed to want to talk about them much.

"I know. I just wish I had a sister I could stand."

"Look, try to make up with her. She's obviously going through a hard time and needs your support. Just because you adjust easily doesn't mean everybody does."

We had reached the room and Francie was waiting by his desk. Before I could say anything she said, "Mark, I've got to talk to you. Can you give me a ride home?"

"Sure," he said. "Just a minute."

"Hi, Jenny," said Francie.

"Hi." I was furious. Couldn't she at least have waited until Mark and I had finished our conversation?

"Jenny, listen, you'd better hurry. Your time in the darkroom has started already. I'll see you on Friday. Meanwhile, try not to worry. Oh, here, give this to your mother."

He handed me an 8x10 copy of the picture of Billy. He had cropped and enlarged it. It was beautiful.

"Mark, it's beautiful. She'll love it. Thanks," I said.

"Talk to you later." He grabbed his books and hurried down the hall after Francie.

Even though he had assured me they were just friends, I couldn't help being jealous. He couldn't work in the darkroom with me, but he had time to talk to her. I wondered what it was she was so anxious to talk about. As I walked back to the darkroom I couldn't get it out of my mind. Images of Mark and Francie in the Volkswagen kept popping into my head.

I had a lot of work to do, and as I began developing I was able to put aside my worries, but even then, a part of my mind was on Mark and Francie. When I saw the pictures of the conference, however, my excitement made me forget everything else. They were good. I had used the techniques we had talked about, and they had worked. My scenery shots were the best I had ever taken. There was one of the view of the mountains and valleys from the lookout point where Mark and I had stood that turned out very well. As I looked at it, I thought about the morning that Mark and I had stood there together, and I told myself I was being silly to be jealous of Francie.

* * * *Chapter Fourteen*

      Thanksgiving morning didn't seem like Thanksgiving at all. Usually we went to Grandma and Grandpa's house, which is outside of Lakeland on a beautiful little pond. It was a forty-minute drive, and we would leave first thing in the morning, and spend the day there. Aunt Sally and Uncle Joe and my cousins Mac and Peter would be there, too, and any other strays that Grandma happened to invite. This year we had talked about going back to Lakeland, but it was an eight-hour drive, and Mom and Dad had decided it would be too hectic. Also, Grandma and Grandpa were coming at Christmas time to see our new house, so we would see them soon anyway. Mom and Dad had decided we would go back to Lakeland in the spring instead.

      Anyway, I woke up late, and though I was happy to

remember that I had four days of vacation coming up, it
didn't feel like Thanksgiving, and for the first time in
over a month I was homesick for Lakeland. I wondered
if Molly was feeling the same way. I thought about
going to her room to talk, but when I went past her door
I saw that it was shut tight. I figured she was still
asleep, or moping about Todd. I remembered how mad
I was at her, and didn't feel like talking anymore. I
went downstairs, got a cup of coffee, and sat down to
read the paper. Mom was making the stuffing for the
turkey.

"It's been ages since I've cooked Thanksgiving
dinner," she said.

"It seems funny to be here and not at Grandma and
Grandpa's," I said.

"I know, but we'll still have fun, don't worry. And
don't forget they'll be coming at Christmas."

"I know, but it won't seem like Thanksgiving with
just us," I said.

"Well, there won't be just us. Remember I told you
that two of Dad's students will be coming. They both
live far from home and didn't have anywhere to eat
Thanksgiving dinner except the dorm, which sounds
grisly, so he asked them along to eat with us."

"Oh, great," I said sarcastically.

"What's wrong? They sound like very nice boys."

"Mmmm. I'll bet." As far as I was concerned,
anyone who wanted to spend their vacation at their
teacher's house had to be a little weird, even if their
teacher was a nice one like Dad. I didn't say this to
Mom, however.

"Need any help with dinner?" I asked.

"Not right now, thanks, sweetie. Have you seen
Molly this morning?" she asked.

"No, I think she's still asleep."

"Well, Dad and I are going to take a drive over to the college and then up to the lake. I thought I'd like to take a nice long walk and get some exercise. Want to come? You could bring your camera."

I didn't have any plans and there was nothing better to do, so I decided I might as well.

"Okay. When are we going?"

"In an hour or so. I have a few things to do first. Billy's coming, too, so why don't you see if you can talk Molly into coming."

I went up to get dressed and knocked on Molly's door.

"Molly, Mom wants to know if you want to take a drive over to the lake?"

"No, thanks," she said.

"Look, everyone else is going, and there's nothing else to do, so you might as well."

"I don't want to," she said.

Well, I tried. I didn't see what else I could do. If she wanted to sit home and mope no one could stop her.

The rest of us piled into the car. We went to the college briefly so Dad could pick up some papers that students had handed in late last night before they left for the Thanksgiving break, and then we drove over to the lake. It was a pretty day. Mom and I took a long walk while Dad and Billy threw a baseball. Mom had brought some sandwiches, and after our walk we sat in the sun by the edge of the lake and ate them. I took some pictures practicing the new techniques I had learned at the conference. It was a nice day and I felt less homesick than I had earlier.

Finally Mom said, "Well, we'd better get back. We

have to get dinner ready. What time are these boys expected?''

''I told them any time after five,'' said Dad as we walked to the car.

At home I helped Mom get dinner ready, and then put on a skirt. I figured I should try to look festive since it was Thanksgiving and we were having guests and all. Molly was still in her room and apparently had been there all day. Dad's students arrived at a little past six, and Mom called up to Molly to come down. She came down in an old pair of jeans, and hardly even bothered to say hello to the two boys when Dad introduced her. I could tell that Mom and Dad were furious, but they pretended not to notice.

Actually, one of the students turned out to be quite nice. He was interested in film making, so we talked a lot about photography, and I found that I liked him. The other was very quiet and didn't seem to have much to say. He played with Billy, trying to be nice, and talked to Dad about his courses, but other than that he was quiet. They both had thirds of everything, so I guess they did appreciate a home-cooked meal.

After dinner Mom asked Molly to get out her guitar, but Molly said, ''I can't play well enough yet. Anyway, I've got homework to do. Nice meeting you,'' she said with a glance at the boys, and then she flounced upstairs without another word.

Dad and Mom looked at each other, and Mom shook her head.

''Molly's having a tough time adjusting to our new home. She really misses Lakeland. I think today is especially hard because we usually spend Thanksgiving with my parents and her cousins.''

''Yeah, I know how she feels,'' said the quiet boy. I

suppose he was feeling a bit homesick, too. Too bad he and Molly couldn't get together and mope, I thought.

They left at around nine, and I was just thinking happily about seeing Mark the next day when the phone rang. It was Mark.

"Listen, I've got bad news. Something's come up and I won't be able to see you tomorrow. My dad's going to be in town, and he wants to spend the day with me. He's only going to be here overnight. I'm really sorry. Can we do it on Saturday instead?"

"That's okay. I understand. We can do it Saturday. I'll miss you tomorrow, though," I said.

"I'll miss you, too, but thanks for understanding. I'll call you tomorrow night."

"All right. Bye."

Well, that blew tomorrow. So far this vacation was not shaping up very well. But I couldn't blame Mark. He hardly ever got to see his father since his parents are divorced and his father lives in Chicago. I couldn't blame him at all. And I would see him on Saturday, so it didn't make too much difference. I needed to spend some time on my project anyway, so I decided I would work hard on it the next day.

It turned out to be another beautiful day, and again it was quite warm for the time of year. I was glad because it meant there would be lots of people out. I wanted to get some pictures of women jogging, roller skating, and biking. Those were sports, too, and I figured they should be included. I ate breakfast and got to the park by ten. There was plenty of activity, and I spent an hour or so happily snapping away. There was a little pond with a jogging track around it, and some benches nearby. I sat down on one to reload my camera, and when I looked across the pond, what I saw almost

caused me to fall off the bench. Mark was sitting there
talking very seriously to Francie. He was holding one
of her hands in his. They were much too far away for
me to hear what they were saying, but it looked like a
heavy conversation. I was so shocked I couldn't even
move for a minute, and then I ran.

I could feel the tears starting to well behind my eyes.
I was terrified Mark or Francie would see me. I knew I
wouldn't be able to talk to them. I ran all the way
home, up the stairs and into my room where I collapsed
on the bed. Mark had sworn that he and Francie were
just friends, so why did he cancel our date to be with
her? And why did he have to make up a story about his
father being in town? It seemed clear to me that he was
just waiting for the right moment to break out of our
relationship so that he could be with her. Lately he'd
been spending more time with her than with me anyway. The tears started running down my face. I let
them come. I lay down and sobbed into my pillow,
hoping no one would hear. Pretty soon the hurt gave
way to anger. If Mark wanted to be with Francie more
than me, fine. I was through. I was tired of playing
second fiddle to a spoiled, mixed-up girl like her.

I lay on my bed for over an hour, going over and over
in my mind what Mark had said on the phone, and what
I had just seen. I wanted to find some excuse. Part of
me couldn't believe that Mark would lie. It just wasn't
like him. But I had seen him with Francie with my own
eyes.

After a while I went downstairs and fixed myself a
sandwich. No one was around. Even Molly was gone.
She had finally emerged from her room. I spent the rest
of the afternoon trying to keep my mind off Mark, but
I was unable to think about anything else. I wondered if
he was going to call as he had said he would. I thought

about what I would say if he did. Should I tell him I had
seen him and Francie or not? Should I give him a
chance to explain?

When he hadn't called by ten o'clock that night, I
figured he wasn't going to. It was obvious to me that it
was all over between us. I was more depressed than
ever. I guess I had secretly hoped that he would call and
explain everything. Every time I thought about him I
felt a lump in my throat, but I was determined not to cry
again. I decided the only thing to do was to go to bed.
Maybe things would look brighter in the morning.

I had just turned off the light when Molly knocked
on my door.

"Yes?" I said.

"Can I come in?" she asked.

"I'm in bed already. I'm really beat. Can it wait?" I
just couldn't face talking to anyone right then.

"Never mind," she said, sounding angry. "Sorry to
bother you."

I felt bad, but I just couldn't cope with anyone else's
problems right then. All I wanted was to be left alone.

I slept badly, and when Mom called me to the phone
at 9:30 the next morning, I was still half asleep. I
thought it was probably Susan, because she had said
she would call. It didn't even occur to me that it would
be Mark.

"Hello," I said into the phone.

"Hi. How are you?" When I heard Mark's voice
panic washed over me. I didn't know what to say.

"Jenny," he said. "Are you okay?"

"I'm okay," I said.

"What's wrong? You sound upset. I'm sorry I
couldn't call last night, but Dad took me out for dinner,
and it was pretty late when we got home. I figured your
parents wouldn't appreciate me calling so late."

"Oh. How was your father?" I asked.

"The same. It was good to see him at first, but then we ended up fighting like always. We can't even spend one day together without arguing."

I couldn't believe he was lying to me like this.

"Mark, I know you didn't see your father yesterday," I said.

"What are you talking about? He got in at one o'clock. We spent the afternoon together and then went out to dinner."

"I saw you with Francie," I said.

"Oh, yeah. She called me yesterday morning and asked me to meet her in the park. She had to talk."

"Oh," I said.

"I just met her for a few minutes, and then I went home to wait for my father. What's the big deal?"

"Well, I thought . . ."

"What did you think? That I'd lied to you?"

"Well, I wasn't sure what was going on when I saw you in the park with her after you'd broken your date with me."

"Look, I told you before. There's nothing but friendship between Francie and me. She's having a lot of problems right now, and she needs someone to talk to. Her parents are getting divorced. I know her parents pretty well since we sort of grew up together, and she knows all about my parents' divorce, so it's easy for her to talk to me about it. I wish you could understand. It's not like you to be so selfish. I'm just trying to help a friend. That's what friends are for, isn't it?"

He sounded angry. I guess he was mad at me for thinking he had lied to me. But I was angry, too. Even if he hadn't lied, I was still tired of playing second fiddle to Francie.

"Well, I'm sorry if I want to see you every once in a

while when you're not too busy administering to your friends."

"Look, let's get together and talk this out," he said.

"Don't you want to check with Francie first and make sure it's okay?" I asked.

"I'll call you later. Maybe you'll have grown up a bit by then," he said, slamming the phone down.

When I went back to my room it was with a mixture of anger and relief. I was relieved that Mark hadn't lied to me, and that he did still care, because no matter how much I might have tried to convince myself otherwise, I still cared very much about him. But I was also angry. Partly with myself, and partly with him. Was I being selfish? I wasn't sure at that point. Why did Francie get to talk to him all the time whenever she felt like it? I had problems, too, but he didn't come running to me every time I wanted to talk. I guessed I had jumped to conclusions when I saw them together in the park. Was there really anything wrong with trying to help a friend? The more I thought about it, the more I realized that I had been wrong. Mark had done nothing wrong, and I had accused him of lying, and then acted jealous and immature when he tried to explain about Francie's parents. I decided I should call him and apologize. But first I wanted to have some breakfast, and figure out what to say. I went downstairs, completely unprepared for what I was about to discover.

* * * *Chapter Fifteen*

     I went downstairs, still thinking about how I should apologize to Mark. Mom, Dad, and Billy were already up. Dad was doing his thing in the kitchen, and Mom was fitting a costume on Billy for a school play. He was supposed to be an elf.

     "Hi, Jen," said Dad. "Breakfast is almost ready. Go on up and tell Molly, will you?"

     I went to the bottom of the stairs and shouted, "Molly, breakfast."

     There was no answer, so I shouted again, and finally I ran upstairs and banged on her door. There was still no answer. I figured she was sound asleep. I opened the door and was surprised to find that her bed was empty.

     "Molly?" I looked around her room. She was gone. I went into the bathroom to see if she was in the shower or something, and then checked the other rooms upstairs. She wasn't there. I ran downstairs. "Molly's not there," I said.

"What do you mean?" said Mom.

"She must have gotten up early and gone for a walk or something," I said.

"I've been up since seven, and it's almost eleven. Where would she have gone?" said Mom, looking alarmed. "Are you sure she's not in the shower?"

Mom went up to Molly's room, and Dad followed her. I went up, too. I was beginning to get a sick, scared feeling in my stomach. Mom looked around her room. Then she went all over the upstairs calling Molly. Finally she checked her closet.

"Her purse and some of her clothes are gone," said Mom. "I think she's run away." She sat down on the bed. Her face was deadly white, and she looked as if she was in shock.

Dad looked at Mom. "But, wouldn't she have left a note or something? I mean, she wouldn't just disappear. Would she?"

They were both on the edge of panic, not wanting to believe this was really happening. I felt the same way. The whole thing didn't seem real, more like a bad dream. It's something you read about, but not something that really happens.

Mom shook her head. "No, I can feel it. She's gone away. The room wouldn't feel like this if she were just out for a walk or something."

I knew what she meant. Molly is very neat, and her room is always the same. Now it was different, as if something was missing.

"Look," I said, pointing to the spot where her pictures of Todd and of our family usually were. "Her pictures are gone. She must have taken them with her."

"Let's not panic," said Dad, who looked as if he were just about to fall apart. "Let's just try to think calmly. If she went somewhere, where would she go?"

"Back to Lakeland," I said.

"Maybe she's gone to your parents," Mom said to Dad. "Maybe we should call them."

"But if she's not there, and I doubt that she is, they'll just worry themselves sick. Let's wait," said Dad.

"What about Todd?" I said. "Maybe she went to see him since he couldn't come here."

"It's possible," said Mom. "Or he at least might know where she is. Shall we call his family?"

The four of us trooped downstairs to the den where Dad began placing a call to the Babcocks, Todd's parents. Billy had started to cry, and looked absurdly pathetic, with his elf's costume half on, the shoes with their turned-up toes and the hat hanging askew from his head. I sat down and pulled him onto my lap. "Don't worry. We'll find her," I said, trying to keep the fear out of my voice.

"Mr. Babcock?" said Dad into the telephone. "This is Bill Whitlock, Molly's father.

"Yes, that's right. No, we live in Stromley, Connecticut, now. Yes, well, actually, the reason I'm calling is that we think Molly has taken a trip back to Lakeland, and we were wondering if she may have gone to see Todd.

"Oh, oh, I see. Ummm, yes. Well, she'll probably go to her grandparents then. Yes, would you do that? Thank you for your help."

Dad hung up the phone looking more upset than ever. "Todd's away for the weekend. With his new girlfriend and her family."

"His new girlfriend? Oh, poor Molly. I wonder if

she knew,'' said Mom.

"Well, let's try my parents,'' said Dad. He put through a call to Grandma and Grandpa, and as we had expected they were worried sick, and, of course, they had no idea where Molly was.

"Do you think we should call the police?'' asked Mom. "She may not have gone to Lakeland at all. We really have no idea where she is.'' As she said this Mom started to cry. I could tell she was making an effort to stay in control, but the idea of Molly's being out there somewhere alone was too much for her.

"It's no good calling the police yet,'' said Dad. "Since she's over thirteen they won't consider her missing until she's been gone twelve hours. She was here at midnight last night when we checked on her before we went to bed. She must have left very early this morning. If we haven't heard anything by noon, we'll call the police.''

"I can't just sit here waiting. There must be something we can do,'' said Mom.

"Wait a minute,'' I said. "What about her friend Ellen Hull? She's been calling her a lot lately, and she's gotten some letters from her. Maybe she knows something.''

"That's an idea. It's worth a try,'' said Mom.

"Okay,'' said Dad. "Let me get their number.''

He got the Hulls' number, and called them and spoke to Mr. Hull, who was a friend of Dad's. He talked for a while, and when he hung up he said, "Eric Hull says that Ellen got a call very early this morning, and went out without saying where she was going. They think it might have been Molly. Eric said he'll call as soon as they hear anything. He said they expect her back shortly.''

"I'm sure she's with Ellen,'' I said. "She must be.''

There was nothing to do but wait by the phone. Mom and Dad discussed calling the police again, but decided to wait until the Hulls called back. At 11:30 the phone rang. Dad answered it.

"Yes, Eric. She is. Oh, thank God. Where are they? I see. Ummhmm, yes. Well, thank you, Eric. Yes, please do." He hung up the phone. "Ellen called. Molly's with her. She wouldn't say where they were, but she's safe. Eric told Ellen to have Molly contact us."

"Oh, thank God," said Mom. "At least we know she's safe."

"Where's Molly?" asked Billy.

"She's with a friend, honey. She's safe. That's all we know right now."

"I'm so glad you thought of calling the Hulls," Mom said to me. "I hope Molly will call us right away. I can't think what's gotten into her. I knew she was unhappy, but to do this." Tears started coming into Mom's eyes again.

I felt a lump in my throat, and suddenly I was crying, too. I ran to Mom and hugged her. "It's my fault," I said. "She asked if she could talk to me last night, but I was still mad at her, and tired and upset because of something with Mark. If only I'd talked to her."

"Now, listen. It's no one's fault," said Mom. "We've all tried to help Molly through whatever it is that's troubling her so, but sometimes people have problems that only they can solve. I won't have anyone blaming themselves."

Even so, I felt terrible every time I thought of Molly knocking on my door last night. If only I'd known.

Dad called Grandma and Grandpa to tell them what we had found out. Then he said, "The only thing we can do now is wait. Eric said he'd have Ellen call us

when she comes home if we don't hear from Molly in
the meantime. Let's not tie up the phone in case she's
trying to reach us. We might as well eat some breakfast
and get dressed. Sitting around in our pajamas won't
do any good.''

Dad had cooked a delicious breakfast. It had all
gotten cold, but he warmed it up. No one could eat
much even so, but we all picked at the food and
pretended to enjoy it. I kept staring at the phone, as if I
could make it ring just by wishing hard enough that it
would.

After breakfast we all got dressed, and then con-
tinued waiting. I kept thinking over and over, if only I
had talked to Molly last night. I tried to remember what
Mom had said about not blaming ourselves, but I
couldn't help it. I thought about my problems with
Mark, and how insignificant they now seemed. If only
Molly would come home safe and sound, I promised
God I'd never be so selfish again.

The phone rang once for Billy, who was told by Dad
to hang up immediately, and once for Mom, who said
she couldn't talk right then. Every time it rang we all
jumped. When it rang a third time, I knew it had to be
Molly. Dad answered and said right away, ''Yes, we
accept.'' He looked at Mom and nodded. ''It's her.''

''Molly, where are you, honey? We've been worried to death,'' said Dad. ''Wait a minute, sweetie.
Start from the beginning. We're not mad. We just want
you home safe and sound. Okay, now calm down. It's
all right, sweetie. Let me get your mother.''

''She's fine,'' he said. ''But very upset. She feels
terrible for having done it. Why don't you see if you
can calm her down.''

Mom took a deep breath and made a visible effort to

compose herself. "Hi, sweetie. Are you all right?"
said Mom in her calm, soothing voice. The same voice
that had picked us up when we had fallen, or comforted
us after a nightmare.

"It's okay. As long as you're safe, that's all that
counts. Let's not worry about that now. Where exactly
are you?"

"Okay, that's not too far from Grandma and
Grandpa's. Do you have any money?"

"Good, when you hang up, call a cab and go to their
house. I'll call them right away and tell them you're on
your way. Call me when you get there and we'll figure
out how to get you home. Are you okay, now? All
right. Call me when you get to Grandma's."

Mom hung up the phone. "Oh, what a relief," she
said. "I'd better call Grandma right away and tell her
Molly will be there in a few minutes." She made the
call, and at the end I heard her say, "Well, that's not a
bad idea. Maybe we will. Let me talk to Bill."

When she hung up Mom said, "What would you
think about driving out there? If we left now we could
be there by eight. We could come back late tomorrow.
It would be a quick trip, but it might be the best thing
for Molly."

Dad thought about it for a minute. Then he looked at
Billy and me. "What do you say, gang? Feel like a
quick trip to Lakeland?"

Molly called when she got to Grandma and Grandpa's house, and we told her we were all coming to
Lakeland. An hour later we had packed everything we
needed, which wasn't much since we were only going
for the night, and we were on our way to Lakeland. We
were almost halfway there when I remembered that I
hadn't called Mark to apologize. I decided I would call

him from Grandma's even though it was long distance.

The drive took almost eight hours, and I had a lot of time to think along the way. I realized how selfish I had been lately, so wrapped up in my own problems that I was unable to see how desperate Molly was. My own problems seemed so small and insignificant now. I thought about what Mark had said about trying to help a friend, and I realized how right he had been. If only I had tried harder to help Molly this might never have happened. I also saw how silly it was of me to be jealous of Mark's friendship with Francie. If her parents were getting divorced, it was no wonder she needed someone to talk to. This thing with Molly had made me realize how devastating family problems can be.

We arrived in Lakeland a little before eight, and as we drove up the drive Molly came running out. Mom jumped out of the car and Molly rushed into her arms. "I'm sorry," Molly sobbed. "I don't know why I did it, but all of a sudden I just felt like I had to get away from Stromley, I thought I wanted to see Todd, but Ellen told me he's with another girl, and you know what, I don't even care. As soon as I got here I realized how dumb I've been lately. I'm sorry."

"Sometimes it takes a drastic move to make us wake up and face reality, honey. You just didn't want to make an effort in Stromley. Now that you know you have to, maybe it'll be easier for you," said Mom.

We all gave Molly a hug, and then we went inside and the round of hugging and kissing began all over again when we saw Grandma and Grandpa. We hadn't seen them since we had left Lakeland at the end of the summer. They were happy to see us all, and I think we were all glad we had come.

Since it was a visit on such short notice, Grandma

hadn't had time to get much food in the house, so Grandpa decided to take us all out to dinner.

"Let's splurge since you're only here for one night," he said. We went to a fantastic restaurant. For dessert they brought around a cartful of all kinds of gooey pastries and cakes. Billy ordered two, and Grandpa said it was okay. As Billy dug into the first, he said, "Boy, this is great. You ought to run away more often, Molly."

"That's not funny, Billy," Mom said sharply. Molly didn't say anything, but she blushed and looked embarrassed. It was pretty obvious that she had put Mom and Dad and all of us through hell. I could tell she felt terrible about it.

Back at Grandma's Mom brought out Molly's guitar which she had remembered to put in the car and asked her to play something for Grandma and Grandpa. We sat around singing and talking until almost midnight. Even Billy was allowed to stay up.

Finally Grandma made us all go to bed. Molly and I were sharing a room.

"Just like old times," I said as we got ready for bed.

"Yeah. Sometimes I miss sharing a room, even though you are a pig," she said.

"A pig, ha. Just because I don't have a neatness compulsion like you. I know what you mean, though. I miss it, too, sometimes."

When I came back from the bathroom Molly was sitting on her bed. "Jenny, I'm really sorry about the way I've been acting lately. I can't really explain what was wrong, but I feel much better now. I think I'll be able to cope with Stromley."

"I'm sorry about our fight, and that I've been so wrapped up in my own problems lately," I said.

"I was kind of hurt that you never seemed to have

time to do anything with me anymore,'' she said. That made me feel so bad. I was determined that from now on I would have time for Molly. We stayed up talking late into the night. She tried to explain to me why she had such a hard time making friends. She seemed to be explaining it to herself as well as to me.

"I'm going to try harder when we get home,'' she said. "There are some nice kids in Stromley. I just haven't given anyone a chance. By the way, how are things with you and Mark?''

I told her everything that had happened between Mark and me. It felt so good to talk, and it helped me straighten things out in my own mind. "Tomorrow I'm going to call him and apologize. I just hope when I explain about everything that's been going on he'll understand. I've never felt this way about anyone before. It's sort of scary in a way,'' I said.

By the time we finally fell asleep Molly and I felt closer than we had all fall. I think we were both determined that this time we'd stay that way. I knew we'd have fights again, but I also knew that I never wanted to get to the point where we couldn't talk things out again.

We both slept in since we had stayed up so late, and were awakened by Billy, who came flying into our room and jumped from one bed to the other.

"Go away. Get out of here,'' I moaned.

"Mom said to get you up,'' he said. "It's almost ten, and Aunt Sally and Uncle Joe and Mac and Peter are coming for lunch.''

We got up and dressed and went downstairs. Mom said we'd be leaving at about four. She told us we could call one or two friends and ask them over after lunch if we wanted to see them.

I did want to call Jody and a few other old friends,

but the first thing I had to do was call Mark. I was very nervous. I wasn't sure how he would react, or if he was still mad, or if he would even talk to me. The last time I had talked to him was yesterday morning before we had discovered that Molly was gone. It seemed like centuries ago.

I went into the den hoping for some privacy. I knew I couldn't talk too long, since it was long distance, but at least I could apologize and explain where I had been. I dialed his number and he answered.

"Mark, it's me," I said.

"Jenny, where are you? I tried to call yesterday and again this morning. There's been no one at your house."

"I know. We're in Lakeland. Listen, before I explain, I want to say I'm sorry for the way I acted on the phone yesterday, and for thinking you lied to me. I was so dumb. I realize that now."

"Well, I'm sorry, too. This whole weekend has been a mess. Here it is Sunday and we haven't even seen each other. Let's just forget all about it and start all over. Why are you in Lakeland?"

"Molly ran away. We'll be back tonight around nine. We just came for one night to pick her up. Everything's fine now, but it was awful for a while. I'll tell you all about it once we're home."

"Okay. I'll call at about nine tonight. I'm glad everything's all right, and, I've missed you."

"Me, too. Bye, Mark."

Molly came in just as I hung up the phone. "That was Mark," I told her. "He's not mad, and I think everything's going to be okay between us."

"I'm so glad, Jenny. That's great," she said, and I could tell she really meant it.

The rest of the afternoon sped by. Our cousins came

for lunch, and then we had a big softball game in which everyone from Grandma to Billy participated. I called Jodie and some of my other friends. Jodie came over for a few minutes just before we left. It was great to see her, even though it was so short. When two o'clock came no one wanted to go, but Dad was adamant, so we all piled into the car. I slept most of the way home.

It was almost ten when we pulled into our driveway, and of course it was dark, so at first I didn't notice the figure sitting on the front steps. Dad said, "Who in the world can that be?" I looked over, and there was Mark.

"I think it's someone for Jenny," said Mom. "Make it fast," she said, looking at me. "I want everyone in bed fast."

I jumped out of the car and ran around to the front steps where he was waiting. When I saw him I was so happy that I put my arms out and hugged him right there. I didn't care who saw us.

"I can't stay," he said. "But I just had to see you. I missed you so much."

"Oh, Mark. I'm so glad you came over. The last few days have been terrible."

We sat on the front steps even though it was freezing cold. I told him everything that had been going on, and everything that I had been thinking, about how selfish I had been with Molly, and how silly I had been about Francie. I explained about discovering that Molly was gone, and the trip to Lakeland, and everything. "It's been awful," I said, "but I've learned a lot."

He didn't say anything for a minute, but just held my hands and looked at me. Then he said, "I've learned something, too. I love you." He kissed me, and I knew he meant it.

"Jenny," Mom called from inside. "You'll have to say good night now."

Mark stood up. "I'd better go, but remember what I said. And next weekend we'll make up for this one."

"Thanks for coming over. And Mark, I love you, too."

I watched as he ran down the walk and got into his car. I had never told anyone I loved them before because I didn't want to say it unless I was sure I meant it, but this time, I was sure.

When a teen looks for romance,
she's looking for

Caprice romances represent the finest in love
stories written especially for you—today's teen!
Filled with the challenges, excitement and
anticipation that make romance so wonderful,
Caprice novels deliver irresistible reading pleasure,
month after month. If you enjoyed this book, treat
yourself, or a friend, to the **Caprice** experience...

Send me:

_____ CARRIE LOVES SUPERMAN #16/09178-4/$1.95
_____ PROGRAMMED FOR LOVE #17/68250-2/$1.95
_____ A NEW LOVE FOR LISA #18/57169-7/$1.95
_____ WISH FOR TOMORROW #19/89446-1/$1.95
_____ THE BOY NEXT DOOR #20/07185-6/$1.95
_____ A HAT FULL OF LOVE #21/31787-1/$1.95
_____ TWO LOVES FOR TINA #22/83380-2/$1.95
_____ LOVE IN FOCUS #23/49630-X/$1.95

Available at your local bookstore or return this form to:

 TEMPO
Book Mailing Service
P.O. Box 690, Rockville Centre, NY 11571

Please send me the titles checked above. I enclose _____
Include $1.00 for postage and handling if one book is ordered; 50¢ per book for
two or more. California, Illinois, New York and Tennessee residents please add
sales tax.

NAME _____

ADDRESS _____

CITY _____ STATE/ZIP _____

(allow six weeks for delivery)   T-10

★ ★ **WIN ★ WIN ★ WIN** **★ ★**

FLY TO HOLLYWOOD AND MEET

GORGEOUS "CHiPs" STAR

BRUCE PENHALL

★ ★ ★ ★ ★ ★ ★ ★ ★ ★ ★ ★

Teaming up with **Super Teen,** the #1 teen magazine for the inside facts, photos, scoops and gossip on all the hottest stars, **Caprice** is ready to offer YOU the dreamy chance of a lifetime! Imagine flying to Hollywood and meeting blond, blue-eyed Bruce Penhall face-to-face! Bruce is the California-born cutie who stars with Erik Estrada on the smash NBC-TV show "CHiPs"! He doesn't have much time for dates between acting, surfing and riding the motorcycle that made him a champion racer...but you could be the lucky one! Just clip the coupon. But hurry...**Caprice** and **Super Teen** can't wait to give this exciting once-in-a-lifetime opportunity away!

I WANT TO MEET
BRUCE PENHALL
IN PERSON!

NAME_____ AGE_____

ADDRESS_____

CITY_____ STATE_____ ZIP_____

**SEND TO
MEET BRUCE PENHALL CONTEST**
CAPRICE
BERKLEY PUBLISHING GROUP, INC.
DEPARTMENT BW
200 MADISON AVENUE
NEW YORK, NY 10016

OFFICIAL RULES

Winner will be selected at random. No purchase necessary. (Alternate means of entry: send information above on a 3" x 5" card to MEET BRUCE PENHALL CONTEST.) Employees of MCA, Inc., and Sterling's Magazines, Inc., including subsidiaries and affiliates, and their families are ineligible to be contestants. Contest void where prohibited by law. All federal, state and local regulations apply. Winner under the age of 18 must be accompanied by parent or guardian. All travel expenses paid.

All entries must be postmarked by August 31, 1983.

SENSATIONAL GIFT IDEAS CAPRICE READERS WON'T WANT TO MISS!

Now that you're reading the best in teen romance, why not make that *Caprice* feeling part of your own special look? Four great gifts to accent that "unique something" in you are all yours when you collect the proof-of-purchase from the back of any current *Caprice* romance!

Each proof-of-purchase is worth 3 Heart Points toward these items available <u>only</u> from *Caprice*. And what better way to make them yours than by reading the romances every teen is talking about! Start collecting today!

Proof-of-purchase is worth 3 Heart Points toward one of four exciting premiums bearing the distinctive *Caprice* logo

CAPRICE PREMIUMS
Berkley Publishing Group, Inc./Dept. LB
200 Madison Avenue, New York, NY 10016

SEND ME THESE FABULOUS *CAPRICE* GIFTS:

Quantity	Item and Individual Price	Amount Due
_____	**Choker(s)** @ $3.25 + 12 Heart Points each	_____
_____	**Ankle Bracelet(s)** @ $3.25 + 12 Heart Points each	_____
_____	**Cosmetics Bag(s)** @ $2.25 + 9 Heart Points each	_____
_____	**Key Chain(s)** @ $.75 + 6 Heart Points each	_____

Postage and Handling Charge
(add $.75 for each item ordered, $1.50 maximum charge)
Total Due $_____

I have enclosed a check or money order for $_____ (which includes postage and handling charge) with the necessary Heart Points for the *Caprice* premiums indicated above.

NAME_____

ADDRESS_____

CITY_____ STATE_____ ZIP_____

Allow 4–6 weeks for delivery. Offer good as long as supply lasts. Void where prohibited by law. All state and local regulations apply.

Residents of New York State add appropriate sales tax.